# Camp Stonetooth

# Camp Stonetooth

## Kingdom Chronicles Book 3

*Jesse Wilson*

# Chapter One

Talcen sat on the couch watching television. The Unicorn incident in the El-roxian Capital was getting attention on the local news, that and the ending of the trial of Pen Kenders. Unicorn outbreaks happened and they weren't anything new.

The only unique spin on it was that Mocra Industries were behind it somehow, allegedly. Talcen wouldn't have been surprised if they were.

"Maybe it really is the end of the world? First the blades, then the Unicorn attack?" Talcen hissed. "All of this nonsense is making me miss my favorite show," he said and was going to throw the remote control against the wall in frustration.

"Come on, you know how it is. When humans mess up and Unicorns attack everyone makes a big deal out of it. Also, I bet Pen gets off clean and easy as all humans tend to do," Ticcen said and sighed as she came from around a corner into the room.

"Yeah, you're right," Talcen replied and sighed. "Oh, Xy, I can't wait to get to camp," he said to himself and stared out the window. The Morglands were as dark as ever. The dim light of the sun barely touching anything.

"Yeah, me either. I wish it was cloudy so we could go outside, that sun is brutal out there," Ticcen said as she looked out the window. "Yeah, you said it. At least we have our Noxite," Talcen said and was tempted to go outside to do something. Anything to break the boredom of being inside, with camp so close, the feeling of restlessness was strong today.

"Also, don't take the Goddess's name in vain, she just might show up," Ticcen replied with a laugh. The older brother shuddered, he was frustrated and forgot that Xy could show up. She might not have appreciated the attention, but with her, according to all the stories it could have gone well, or terribly.

"Okay fine, you're right," Talcen replied and turned up the television. The commercial came to an end.

"The jury is going to come back with their verdict in minutes. The world will learn the fate of alleged traitor Pen Kenders and –" the power went out and everything went black. "Man, I can't even watch the annoying thing, this sucks," Talcen said and threw the remote down on the couch.

"Damn, well, I'm going to get a snack, do you want anything?" his sister asked and he sighed. "Do we have any bloodstones left?" he asked and she nodded. "Yep, we have a couple," she said and walked off.

"I'm so sick of bloodstones, and everything else," he said and threw his head back into the couch. "Before you know it, we'll be drinking blood and be given the blessing to walk outside at will. Just one more day and we get all of that started. Stop complaining already," she replied as she walked back into the room.

She fell into the couch and tossed him a red crystal. He caught it without looking and in the same motion he sank his fangs into the side of it.

Bloodstones were what all neophyte vampires were forced live on until they went through their training, the rite of passage or whatever the council called it. It tasted like blood flavored with metal and it wasn't very filling. He couldn't wait to taste actual warm blood for the first time.

The thought of it was almost enough to distract him from the taste of the horrid fluid from this stone. Almost being the key word. He finished it and the red stone was clear and empty. He tossed the empty stone against the wall and it shattered.

"What the hell, man, why did you do that?" she asked him and jumped as it broke. "Who cares, you know the crystals just dissolve in the air anyway, so who cares?" he replied and didn't like her always nagging him about the most pointless things.

"I care, the shards don't always go away and when I step on them, it really pisses me off," she replied and glared. "Do you know how long it takes to pull these shards out of your feet, do you?" she asked and kept glaring.

"No, because they go away. I've never stepped on one and I don't know how you manage to do it at all," he said and was getting in a bad mood. Everything was getting on his nerves. He just wanted to go to the last training camp and be allowed to drink blood and get access to the whole reason vampires were clearly superior to the rest of the races in the world.

"Well, think of it this way, once we go through the camp, we never have to go to another one, aren't you going to miss this, even a little bit? It wasn't all bad," she said and held her empty crystal in the palm of her hand as it dissolved in front of her eyes.

"No. Not even a little bit," he replied.

Sitting here in the dark, the world outside seemed to disappear. The sunlight all but shut the Morglands down. Most of the other vampires stayed home and there were still many hours left. Then the phone rang on the end table beside him. He picked it up and pushed the answer button.

"Hello," he said.

"Yeah, come on, the sun is out. We can't go out right now and neither can you," he replied and this got her attention. "I'll ask her," he said and put the phone down. "Boron wants to know if we want to come over," he said. Ticcen looked around, the power was out and there was no telling when it would come back on.

Ever since Mocra had their disaster, the power wasn't reliable. "Oh, what the hell, let's get out of here," she replied and he smiled as he picked the phone back up.

"Sure, we'll be right over," he said and waited for a quick moment. "Yeah, see you later," he said and hung up. "I'll go get the Noxite," he said and stood up slowly. He threw the phone to her. "Catch," he said and laughed. She wasn't expecting it and fumbled it as she did her best to catch it. It fell to the floor.

"Damn it," she said and picked it up. She checked the screen and had a sigh of relief when she saw that it wasn't broken. "This is super expensive. Please try not to throw it, okay?" she asked and he just smirked as he walked away to get the Noxite.

"Good talk," she replied and rolled her eyes in frustration. Her brother was a nightmare to deal with now. How in the world was he going to be when he was granted Xy's blessing? It was impossible to say exactly. She was just glad that living with him was going to be a thing of the past in a few short days.

She stood up as soon as he came back with the Noxite pendant. Like everything else of value, he tossed it to her, not wanting to take the extra steps to hand it to her. She caught it because by now, the past twenty years, she had grown accustomed to this laziness from him.

"Did Boron say if he had a reason for wanting us to come over or was it just a random thing?" she asked him and he just shrugged. "I don't know, he sounded the same as he ever does," he replied and put the pendant around his neck. She did the same thing.

"Oh well, it sounded like he still had power at least," he said and walked to the door, opened it. To anyone not a vampire, the Morglands in the middle of the day would have seemed dark and depressing. However, to young vampires like them even this amount of light was still painful to the eyes. The Noxite pendant began to glow a dull blue as the dim rays of light hit it.

The damaging effects of the light were canceled out but it was still difficult to see for them both as they walked outside.

"I got the keys," he said and she figured he did. He loved to drive. The walked to their green car and he pushed the button to unlock the door. She opened the door and got in. The windows were made of Noxite too and tinted. Her eyes stopped burning when she closed the door. Talcen got in too and rubbed his red eyes as he closed the door. "Just a few seconds," he said as he recovered from the light outside. Then he put the keys in, started the car.

"Alright, and we are off," he said, she rolled her eyes. "Do you have to always narrate everything you do? I'm literally right here. I know we're off," she said and was annoyed.

"I guess not, I just. I don't know. It's a habit okay," he replied and rolled his eyes. He knew he was annoying sometimes but most of the time he didn't even realize the things he said. Sometimes it was just in his head, other times it was out loud and telling the difference was not always easy.

"Yeah, I guess. Let's just get there. All this time outside in the day is driving me nuts," she replied and looked out the window.

It was a cool, calm day. All the excitement in the world was a thousand miles away. She dreamed what it had to be like being on the frontlines of a Unicorn outbreak or the Blade Apocalypse where the details were still coming in over the news, more every day.

Here in the Morglands, existence had been the same as always. Even if the King and Queen had been held hostage by the Mist Blade, everything turned out just fine. Everything was always just fine and boring as it had been.

Talcen drove off down the road, between the quiet houses. The village of Muid was small, typical and like most other places in the Morglands, abandoned in the daylight hours. Boron's house wasn't very far from their own, but in the daylight, traveling by car it felt like forever. What little powers they had, in the daylight, abandoned them.

"At least we don't half to walk," Ticcen said and Talcen looked at her. "If we had to walk we never would have made it. Noxite only lasts for a few hours and we are both super slow walkers. We would have just would have stayed home," he replied and she wondered how vampires ever got along before the invention of cars.

The Morglands must have been much more depressing than they were now, she thought.

Talcen took a left and soon Boron's house could be seen in the distance. It wasn't anything special. Just a one story, small house. Boron was standing outside. He was a tall, skinny elf, but a vampire like the rest of them. The Morglands were a unique part of the world. Almost anyone could be a vampire, but once they were, what they used to be no longer mattered.

Talcen pulled to the side of the street, shut the car off. Both of them got out at the same time. "Well, it's my favorite trolls," Boron said and smiled. "Have you been waiting outside for us the whole time?" Ticcen asked and Boron shook his head.

"No, I just got out to see if you were here yet. You're not that far away after all," he replied. It was about then Ticcen noticed the elf still had power.

"Generator, you shouldn't be without one in these turbulent times," he said and stepped inside. "Come in. I have something I think you're going to want to see," he said with a smile and the two of them just looked at one another.

"A surprise. It's not another gel fiend, is it?" Ticcen asked him and he laughed in response. "No, nothing like that this time. I could hardly believe it," Boron replied and motioned them to come inside. The two of them were happy to get out of the overbearing sunlight and stepped inside.

# Chapter Two

The three of them were inside and Boron was leading them through the house. "It's in the back, you got to see this," he said with an increasing amount of enthusiasm and speed as they walked. It was clear whatever it was, wasn't in the house at all as they headed towards the large sliding door to the back of the house.

Boron slid the thing open and walked right back out. The two followed him and they couldn't believe what was laying on the ground in front of them.

"You found a Grave hound?" Ticcen asked and she backed off, a little afraid. "You're damn right I did. It's even intact, too," Boron said with a big smiled. "Where did you find this thing?" Talcen asked and really wasn't feeling brave enough to get too close, even if it was inactive. "I found it on the outside. It was just lying there out in the open beyond the wall," he replied.

"You went outside? You know that's forbidden," Ticcen replied in disgust. Only bad things existed outside of the walls. She didn't even want to know how he got it back home. "Yeah. I know, but look at this thing," he replied and continued. "The only thing it's missing is the soul crystal. I looked and couldn't find it. A collector is going to pay tons of money for this thing," he said and crossed his arms.

"Or the patrol is going to do a fly over and see it. It's a grave hound. It's kind of hard to miss," Talcen replied and shook his head a little. "I got the cover to hide it, so I'm not worried," Boron replied. All of them were thankful that it wasn't active.

The Grave hound laid on the ground, it was nothing more than a giant dog skeleton. They usually stood about eight feet tall. "It must be over a hundred years old, I didn't think any were left," Ticcen said and Boron shrugged. "I found it lying there like it was sleeping or someone left it there. One quick levitation spell and some quick feet. I had it back here in no time at all," Boron said.

"Wait, it was sleeping?" Talcen asked and took a step back. "Yeah. All curled up. I spread it out just to see how big it really was," Boron replied and then his mind went to the same thing that Talcen was likely thinking. "Oh, hell. You don't think this is some crazy necromancer's pet, do you?" Boron asked, all the sudden he became very nervous about having this thing so close.

"But you said it didn't have a soul crystal, so it can't activate without it," Ticcen said, but that information didn't make anyone feel any better. "True but, still. Whoever owns this thing will come looking and necromancers are usually insane. And if it's here, that means it likely has a tracking spell on it," Talcen suggested.

"Well, okay. Maybe we should just go back inside and maybe who ever owns it will just come find it. Take it and not say anything. If it's still here in a couple of days, I'm going to try and sell it and make enough money to never worry about money again," Boron said, still hopeful that he just got lucky and didn't steal a necromancer's pet.

Even if it was just a mindless war machine. Necromancers got quite attached to their dead things. Grave hounds were not supposed exist anymore. Boron became increasingly afraid. "Well let's just go inside," he said was the first one to go back into the house. "Right," Talcen agreed and the two of them went back inside with him and slid the door close as they did.

"Well, who's excited for Stone tooth?" Boron asked as he sat in his chair. "This guy is," Ticcen replied and pointed at her brother. "Yeah. I can't wait to get the blessing and start existing," he said and sat on the couch. "Then we can get jobs and be proper cogs in the machine, I can't wait to be a cog. That's going to be so much fun," Boron replied to him with a groan.

"What do you mean, you have a job now," Ticcen replied and Boron shook his head. "Yeah but no one expects anything out of you. Unlife is good. Now after this we will be expected to do, you know, more," Boron replied. Ticcen just rolled her eyes.

"You two have barely passed any of the trials of the other camps. What makes you think you can pass Stone Tooth? I've heard it has the hardest trials of all," she said and the two of them looked at one another.

"Stories to scare newbies. Every single camp is the always the worst one ever. It's always the same. No one ever loses. Everyone passes. It's not like the olden days where failure meant extermination. You just keep trying until you pass," Talcen said, he knew full well that if it was the old days, he wouldn't be sitting here right now.

He had to thank the new king every day for that.

"Stone tooth will be over before we know it. We'll be free of this twenty year probation period and then we can do whatever we want. Hell, you could even be a knight if you wanted," Boron said. Talcen laughed. "Me, a knight. I don't think so. I'd be a really bad knight," he replied. He tried to imagine it, him in a suit of armor and failing miserably. He banished the thought.

"How did that Kenders case turn out? The power went out at our place," Talcen figured he'd ask, at least ask. He was forced to watched it this whole time he might as well know how it ended. "Nope, no idea," Boron replied. "I've been on the net most of the time and just watching other stuff. I don't pay attention to real world crap, you know that," he replied to them Talcen just sighed in disappointment but it wasn't terrible.

He didn't care that much. "Oh well, I guess it doesn't matter how it turned out, it doesn't affect me either way," he said and then there was a knock on the front door. "Are you expecting someone else?" Talcen asked and they went quiet. The knock came again, a little louder this time. "No," Boron replied.

Ticcen tensed up. There was a Grave hound in the back yard and they had just got done talking about a necromancer. Now a knock on the door. Is there anyone else it could have been? Her mind started to run away with her. "I'll go see who it is. It could be anyone," Boron said, swallowed as he stood up and walked towards the door.

"If it's the necromancer we're running out the back," Talcen whispered. "What about Boron?" his sister replied. "Screw him he brought the necromancer on himself," Talcen replied and almost smiled. He didn't want to leave his friend behind, but his friend was stupid enough to bring home a necromancer's pet or its personal assassin.

Footsteps started coming back down the hallway and the two of them started to tense up. Boron came down the hall and a shorter figure was behind him. It was a cop. "Hey, kids. I'm Officer Denhar. Nice to meet you. Where's the undead monster?" he said. The man was a human vampire. His eyes were red and skin was pale.

"I'll never tell, no I won't. It's mine and I'm going to make lots of money on that thing," Boron said and his eyes flashed toward the two of them.

"Listen. I know it's close by. If I found it, the Necromancer who it belongs to won't be far behind. Where is it, now," he said again. "Hey, cop. How do we know you're not the necromancer and once we tell you, you'll just dust us anyway," Talcen asked, he had a sudden boost of bravery that came out of nowhere.

"Hey, kid. If I was a necromancer you'd all be dead by now. I'd have no reason to knock on the door, now would I?" he said and raised a good point. None of them had ever heard of a polite necromancer before. "It's in the back. It's in the back, take it," Ticcen said, she didn't want to get into trouble because of two idiots trying to lie to the cops.

Denhar looked towards the back sliding door. "Thanks," he said as he walked around Boron and to the back. He looked out the window and saw it lying there on the ground. "Good," he said and took the radio from inside his long coat.

"Yeah I'm going to need an isolation unit out at my location and a transport. I have three that need a ride to the station who need to answer some questions," he said into it. "Got it, we're on the way," a voice responded.

"Hey, three? We only saw it just before you did. Why do we have to go too?" Talcen asked and Delhar shot a glance at them. "You didn't answer my questions and its procedure," he replied but never looked at the two of them, keeping his eyes on the dormant weapon in the back as if it was going to get up at any moment and kill them all.

"Trust me, it's procedure and it's not like you newbies have anything to do in the next couple of weeks anyway," Delhar replied to them. "Yeah, we actually do. We're taking the Stone tooth trials tomorrow, leaving just after the sun goes down. We can't be in some cell," Boron replied to him and it sounded more like a whine than anything else to anyone who was listening.

The cop's red eyes looked at them. "Stone tooth, eh. So, you live around here then I assume?" he asked them. "Yeah, we live close. You've got to believe us. All we did was come over, we haven't been here more than twenty minutes before you got here," Ticcen said, but tried to keep her voice to not sound like she was begging or anything. There was still a dim chance they weren't going to get taken away to get asked questions neither of them knew the answer too.

Delhar stared at the three of them. "Stone tooth is a pretty big deal. Alright. You three will be questioned when you get back," he said and picked up his radio. "Cancel the transport unit, we'll just take the Hound for now," he said into it. "Got it," a voice replied and was unquestioning in its tone. "You three might not make it back, so just quick. Where did you find this thing?" Delhar asked them. Boron shook his head.

"Fine, I went outside and it was just lying there. As if it was uncovered by the sand or something," he said. "Then I used a levitation spell and brought it home. It didn't even have a soul crystal or anything in it. The dog thing couldn't get up even if it wanted to," Boron said and shrugged. "I thought it was harmless and an easy way to make some money," he said.

Delhar nodded then. "All of you newbies are the same. You all want easy money so you risk your eternal essence to get it. Going outside, you're crazy. However, if you live through Stone Tooth and after all this is over let me know. I may have a job for you," Delhar said and listened as the sounds of a truck pulled up outside.

"Does this mean we can go home?" Ticcen asked and the officer rolled his eyes. Just give me your name and information and yes, you can go home. I'll be contacting you when you get back," he replied. Boron still looked nervous about something. Delhar was eyeing him.

"Is there something you want to say to me?" the cop asked him. "No, I. Well, I just feel really stupid about all of this now. I mean, who would have bought a grave hound anyway?" he asked and looked to the floor. "Necromancers who'd just kill you once they got what they wanted," Delhar replied and shrugged.

"Necromancers aren't exactly the best business people, you know? In all my years doing this job I don't think I've ever met one who's actually paid. They are pretty death happy. I mean, it's literally in their name," Delhar said as the front door opened. Two figures walked through dressed in black robes and didn't pay any attention to the four in the room.

The walked right to the backyard to the hound. They watched as the two mysterious figures waved their hands over the skeleton, mutter some kind of alien words. The skeletal hound disappeared and so did they in a bright blue light.

"I'll be back, Boron. You and your friends have good luck at Stone Tooth. And if you survive, remember. I'll be waiting," Delhar said to them, turned and walked himself out.

# Chapter Three

"Holy Snozbucket, that was close," Boron said as the door closed and he let loose a sigh of relief. "The both of you owe me because you were this close to going to jail instead of going to Stone Tooth, you're welcome," TIccen said to them and her brother almost wanted to give her a big hug right then and there, but he resisted.

"As soon as we can go to a blood bar, I'm buying you the first drink," Boron said with a big smile. "And the second one is on me," her brother said with a smile.

"Well, I don't know. But I've had one excitement for one day. Let's go home and get ready to get for the last training camp we'll ever need to go to," Ticcen said and stood up. She didn't want to be here anymore. Anything to do with the cops or necromancers and that was more than enough for her. Boron was more her brother's friend than hers anyway.

She always just came along for the ride and usually had to sit through a video game session or something like that. "Yep, I'll see you all tomorrow," Boron said to them as they all stood up.

If they were still alive, they might have felt weaker than they did. Being a vampire had its perks, the physical effects of emotions no longer applied. But the mind didn't forget how it felt. Talcen and Ticcen quickly made their way to the door and back to the car. Their Noxite began to glow in the dull sunlight and did its best to protect them both. Boron waved them off and shut the door.

"That was the most insane thing that I've ever had to go through," Talcen said as they got into the car. "Yeah, this is why I like to stay home, twenty-one years of being a vampire and we've managed to avoid the law until a day before the blessing is earned. What stupid luck is that?" Ticcen replied and closed the door.

"Ours, I guess hopefully it's the last time we have to deal with it," Talcen replied and he started the car and drove away.

Ticcen looked out the window. She was sure that there was going to be a figure watching them. A necromancer waiting on the side of the road. No one was there. Maybe the hound was just a relic after all. Of course, she, or many others had any idea how necromancers really worked. She hadn't even bothered to watch a documentary on them or anything. They could still be being watched right now.

The very thought of it made her nervous and all she wanted to do was go home. Thankfully they were weren't far away.

Their house appeared and all the lights were on, shining through the windows. "Either we didn't shut anything off, or, or we have a visitor!" Talcen said trying to sound spooky. "No, moron. When the power goes out I don't know anyone who goes around and shuts all the lights back off," she replied and punched him in the arm lightly.

He was always like this. It was funny when she used to think that the undead were some of the scariest things this world had to offer, now that she was one, the world became much bigger.

The car came to a stop in the driveway and the two of them got out, walked to the front door. It was locked just how she left it and she opened it. Sure enough, she was right. Nothing had been moved, nothing changed. The TV was still on.

"Kenders has been found not guilty on all charges," an ecstatic voice on the television said in pure disbelief as the two of them walked inside.

"Great, another miserable human does major damage and gets away with it," Talcen said as he heard the news. Before he was a vampire, he was a troll. Humans in their eyes were always getting away with something. He shut the door. Ticcen looked at the time and the dim sunlight was getting brighter outside.

"It's time for bed anyway," she said and glanced out the windows that were darkening on their own to protect them.

"The sun even rises in the Morglands. At least it's only bright for a couple of hours until it rises above the clouds," Talcen said, mostly to himself and shut of the television. "I'm actually all ready for Stone Tooth. All I have to do is get up and go," Talcen said, almost like he was proud of the fact.

"No one cares, go to bed," Ticcen replied and started to walk off towards her room. "Well, I care," he replied as she walked into her room and shut the door behind. He took one last look at the rising sun and took off his Noxite pendant off, set it on the table.

The windows were darkening, but the rays of light still burned his skin slightly all the same. "Goodnight, Sun," he said and part of him, even all this time later still kind of missed it. But he always felt this way at sunrise, just a little bit. The glass turned black and he shut the light off. Then as he went to his room shut the rest of them off one at a time.

His bed was a mess, just how he left it when he woke up last night. He threw his clothes off into the corner of the room in a heap, turned the light off and went to bed. He'd nearly forgotten what outside life was like in the daytime for other races anymore. That was just the way he wanted it. It was a nice thought as he closed his eyes and let the day sleep take him again.

# Chapter Four

Time is meaningless in the day sleep, vampires call it that to try their best to remain normal, acceptable to the outside world. It's just another word for death. Hours passed in no time at all. Talcen's eyes snapped open at once and he knew the sun was setting. Setting and that his tenure as a neophyte was at the beginning of the end. He sat straight up and got out of bed in one fluid motion.

"Today is the day," he said and got dressed with the last fresh clothes he had. A red t-shirt and black jeans. He heard the familiar noises of his sister downstairs. Neither of them knew why, but she always woke up just before the sunset and he did during it.

He picked up his bag that he had packed for the trip, opened the door and started to make his way to the living room. The brown bag his sister packed was already by the door. "Welcome back," she said to him as he yawned. "Thanks," he replied.

"What are you doing?" he asked. "I'm just cleaning up. I don't want to come home to a mess, you know it's always better to party in a clean house," she replied as she put the last plate away and closed the cupboard.

"Yeah I hear that. The bus to camp leaves in an hour so we should be on our way," Talcen said and she rolled her eyes. "Yeah, yeah. Fifteen minutes away from the bus and you want to be their early. I get it," she replied and started to walk towards the door. She was always amazed at how much energy he had trying to get to these things, but once he got there, it all disappeared usually.

"Hey, remember the bus to Camp Bane. We had the same attitude and were damn near late. I don't want to risk that again so if you don't mind. I'd rather be early for the last one. After this, you can do whatever you want," he said and Ticcen narrowed her eyes.

She was going to remind him that they were almost late because he couldn't find the keys. But decided against it a fight wasn't worth it right now.

"Do you know where the keys are?" he asked and checked his pockets. Ticcen groaned with an increasing amount of fury.

"So, help me if you lost the keys again I will put the nearest stake through your heart and leave it there for days," she said without thinking about it.

"God damn, woman, calm down, I was kidding. I hung them up where I always do," he replied and didn't want to be staked. "Camp Transcendence was enough of a bad memory," Talcen was reminded of how it felt to be staked, turned to ash and feeling like he was on fire. He still never believed that the experience was only a few seconds, it felt like hours.

Ticcen smiled, she wasn't making an empty threat. Sure, staking one of your own kind was highly illegal in the Morglands but if no one found the body there wouldn't be a crime. She often wondered how many staked skeletons were hiding behind closed doors every single day.

"Well, let's go," she said and walked right past him and out the door into the fresh night air. She looked down the road and saw others coming outside, some going to work and others just enjoying the new night for the first time.

The night never seemed to last as long as the day time around here. But all the same they would all make the most of it. The two of them threw their bags in the backseats and got into the car. "And away we go," Talcen said as he started the car and drove off.

She rolled her eyes at his narration, but let it go.

"I heard permanent death is possible at Stone Tooth. Not everyone makes it out," Ticcen said and her brother shook his head. "No, that's true anymore. The king outlawed any form of true death in all the camps," Talcen said, he was pretty sure he was right about this one and nodded as he turned a corner.

She wasn't convinced, not really. "How many are attending?" she asked. "I don't know. A lot I suppose. But this camp is completely different. I don't know what they plan to do with us, this time around," he replied and accelerated the car a little.

"Well I don't expect any of this to be easy. All I know is that I can't wait to taste real blood," Talcen said and imagined it or tried to. All he knew was the taste of those bloodstones and he hated them, he hated all of the restrictions that he had to go through. He hated so that it was driving him insane, at least he thought it was.

"Easy, none of this has been very easy but as long as we look out for one another, I think we will be just fine," Ticcen replied, trying to sound as sure as she could. The two of them agreed silently and passed another row of houses. "Thankfully the traffic isn't too bad yet," Talcen said trying to make small talk but his sister wasn't paying attention. She was just looking out the window.

"Right," he said to himself realizing that he was just talking to himself now.

The trip didn't last very long and soon enough they were at the bus stop. Lots of other cars were here already. Lots of vampires like them, lots of vampires they didn't recognize, some they did. Boron was there too, waiting for the bus in the distance with all the others.

"See what I mean about getting here early, everyone else had the same idea as I did," he said and smiled as he found a place to park. "Damn, there must be at least forty people here or more," she said and wasn't sure what was going on. All of the other camps were about half this size, at least.

The two of them got out and got their bags. As they walked closer to the station. "Wow, this must be the latest you two have ever been," Boron's voice said to them from the crowd. The two of them were thoroughly confused at what that meant.

"Everyone knows the busses to Stone Tooth can arrive any time after sunset and leave. There isn't any schedule. The number of stories of people who missed the bus are insane," he said and honestly, neither of them knew that.

"Well I'm just glad we made it on time," Talcen said and tried not to feel embarrassed. For someone so excited for this, he realized how little he knew about it. "Me too," Ticcen said and looked around. Every race was represented here, at least from what she could see from here. Vampirism knew no bounds when it came to the genetic barrier.

It was nice to be part of something like this at times like these with so much insanity going on in the world lately. A little normalcy was something everyone could use right now.

Then another noise came out of the dark. The droning engines of the busses. The busses were black with red wheeled rims. 'Camp Stone tooth' was plastered on the sides of them in bright green paint that seemed to glow under the electric light.

"Don't worry, that's all part of the show. I did plenty of research. They just want to set a good mood," Boron said and Talcen wished he would have done more than just assume he knew how everything worked because all the other ones were close to the same thing over and over again.

There were four black, busses and their doors swung open all at the same time. White fog came rolling out the doors and into the crowd at their feet. No one ventured forward just yet. "All aboard to Stone Tooth," a booming voice came out over the crowd and it was only then that they started to move toward the busses.

"We should stick together," Boron suggested to them and Ticcen really didn't want to be on a bus with no one she knew. If they got separated at camp, that was one thing but she was going to do her best to avoid that as long as she could.

"I like that idea, stick together," Talcen agreed with him and the three moved closer together as they moved forward. Sometimes in a crowd, weird things happened in seconds. Boron lead the way and stepped forward on the bus. The driver of the bus was not alive. A skeleton sat behind the wheel and it didn't react to anything or anyone who walked past it. "Really, an animated is taking us to camp," Ticcen said as she walked past it.

"It could be worse, I suppose. Let's just hope the magic doesn't fail half way to the place," Talcen replied and stepped past it. It didn't matter where they sat but Boron walked as far as he could to the back and took the first empty seat he could. "You're sitting with me or with him, but one of us is sitting with a stranger," Talcen said to his sister. "I'll sit with you," she replied and with that he turned to the seat across from Boron and sat down, slid to the window.

She followed him and quickly let the others pass by. "Oh, this is going to be the best trip ever. I get to sit next to the hottest vampire troll on the bus," Boron said and smiled.

"Yeah, but if you're not careful this hot vampire is going to make the rest of your trip very miserable, so watch it," she said and narrowed her eyes. "Okay, geeze. I was just making conversation. Not a big deal. I'll be careful," he replied in a hurry.

"Is this seat saved for someone or can I sit here too?" a female voice said and Boron looked up. "Um, yeah sure," Boron said and stood up. "You can have the window seat," he finished and she smiled at him. Of course, even at his full height he was just in line with her shoulder. He had to look up to see her smile.

A giantess vampire, of course. Even with the crystal around her neck to reduce her size considerably, she was still huge.

"Thank you," she replied and stepped inside, sat down. Boron did too a second later. The enchanted bus seat just expanded in size for the both of them so they could be comfortable. Boron hardly noticed it.

Immediately his attention was shifted to the one beside him. "So how long have you been a vampire?" he asked her. She didn't plan on having a conversation or anything. "Same as all the rest of you here I assume. It is the requirement, right?" she replied and Boron nodded. He should have known that. She was making him a little bit stupid but he'd never been this close to a giantess before.

As vampires went, they were pretty rare. "I guess so, yeah," he replied and looked down. "I'm Boron, what's your name?" he asked.

She turned to look at him. "I'm Nari, if you must know. Listen, I know you've likely never seen anyone like me before, but don't go stupid. Please. You look like you're a smart guy so don't go and prove yourself wrong," she replied to him and Talcen laughed.

"You'll have to forgive my friend. He's always been this way around beautiful women. He loses it. You'll just have to punch him if he doesn't stop. I won't say anything if you do," Talcen added to the conversation.

Nari had to admit to herself that these two might not be completely hopeless and she let her guard down a little. "Alright. Try anything and I'll take you both down at the same time. So, are you guys scared about this last trip?" she asked and the two of them looked at one another. "Yes, they are terrified, I'm Ticcen, this oaf's sister, twins I guess, but you'd never know that," Ticcen said right away and interjected herself into the conversation.

"Nice to meet you," Nari said with as friendly a smile as she could manage. Ticcen nodded and continued. "Yeah. I think everyone one here is a little scared. It's the last trial and I'm sure we've all heard stories from others about this place," she said and the others nodded. "An elder vampire told me that back in her day. Stone Tooth killed the unworthy. That's how they used to maintain the population," Nari said and the other three got nervous.

"Hey, did anyone ever find out why they called it Stone Tooth, anyway?" Boron finally got his wits together enough to ask. "Yeah, I know why," Talcen said. It was about then that the sound of the bus doors closing became apparent. The various conversations came to a stop and the engine roared to life.

"Welcome, I hope all of you are comfortable," a voice came out of the speakers. It was grainy and sounded as if this recording had been played a thousand times over. "The windows will be blacked out, as the location of Stone Tooth is a secret, but do enjoy the trip," the voice said and faded out at the end. The windows, as the voice said, went black just as the bus started to move forward. There was a slight cheer that came out of the crowd but it didn't last long.

"So, anyway," Talcen said and continued. "Back in the day when war golems were all the rage, armies would flood the battlefields with them. Anyway, I heard that there was a particularly effective vampire killing golem made of stone or bone that was near unstoppable. What they did to stop it? They threw it into a lake. It couldn't swim out and it was so heavy that it got stuck in the mud," Talcen said and the story made the others feel as if they couldn't believe such a stupid story was even made up. "Then they managed to take control of it, and set it loose on vampires. Anyone who escaped got Xy's blessing, anyone who didn't, well, their ashes are still out there," Talcen said his short tale.

"I'm not sure where you came up with that. But that was the dumbest story I've ever heard," Boron replied and the others just nodded their heads in agreement. "Well, I didn't see you coming up with anything better. It could be anything at all. If you have something better I'd like to hear it," he replied.

"I've heard a hundred different stories. Everything from that insane golem story you told to it was where Xy herself first touched down and created the first vampire. When you have a place so secret any story can apply and be correct. I don't think anyone really knows what the deal is. But I bet they have a killer story to try and scare us from even attempting to figure it out once we get there," Nari said and looked at the black window.

"I guess we'll see once we all get there," Ticcen said and wondered how long the drive would take. It could be an hour, it could be three days. No details were ever given besides to where the meet the busses. "Well, I'm going to listen to music, let me know when we get there," Nari said, reached in her bag and pulled out her square Silverwave, unraveled the headphone wires and slipped the thing over her head, pushed the button.

Boron waited until she was good and distracted. "Okay, guys I need to come clean," he whispered to them. "What, clean about what?" Talcen said in his normal voice and he quickly quieted him down.

"The grave hound wasn't as empty when I found it," he said and the two of them began to feel nervous. "Dude, what are you talking about?" Talcen asked, this time much quieter. But he knew the answer in his dead heart. It was right there, twisting like a dying snake, but he didn't want to say it. Neither of them did.

"The hound still had its soul crystal resting inside, but the thing wasn't active, it was loose or something. I took it out because I could sell them separately, but when that cop showed up I had to hide it," Boron said and now the two of them knew they were in trouble.

"And where did you hide it?" Ticcen asked him. Boron patted his bag. "I brought it with me. I didn't want those cops searching my place after I left and finding it. I didn't want to give it to you because they are searching your place right now as we speak I bet," he said and smiled.

"So, I hope that you didn't have anything illegal or hiding any secrets," Boron said and Talcen wasn't as far as he was aware, but he wanted to punch him in the face right now.

The only reason he didn't was because he didn't want to cause a scene.

"When all of this is over and we're not in jail, you owe me, big," Talcen said and Ticcen leaned back in her seat. "Well, I guess they are going to find that guy I staked ten years ago in the basement," she said as calmly as she could.

"What?" Talcen asked in horror and she held that straight face for a few seconds. "I'm just kidding. There isn't anyone in the basement," she said and tried to laugh, but the situation wasn't going to get any better. "Not anymore at least," she added and her brother cringed at the thought of going to jail for being associated with something like that.

"Guys, don't worry. As soon as we get to camp I'll ditch the crystal in a place no one will ever find it, I promise," he said and this didn't convince anyone that they were safe. For all they knew as soon as they got off the bus all of the stuff they brought with them would be taken and searched. The rules for each camp was completely different.

"You better, even better yet just be the last one off the bus and leave it here, roll it to the very back and it could have been anyone's after that," Ticcen suggested but Boron sneered at the thought. "No way, if I'm going to get rid of it, I'm going to do it my way," he said and turned away from them.

"Oh Xy, help us," she replied to that response quietly and took herself out of the conversation.

"All the sudden I'm glad we were able to get out of town," Talcen said and his sister just nodded. It was about then she had realized that she lost track of time. The bus was still moving, but she just leaned back into her seat as far as she could and did her best to pretend that she wasn't a part of any of this. That idiot Boron was going to ruin their chances at getting through camp, somehow, she just knew it.

# Chapter Five

The bus ride lasted for hours. With no light besides the dim running lights on the edges of the aisle and nothing changing besides the occasional movement in the distance. Everything was getting boring and Ticcen could only think about all the cops wrecking the place she had worked so hard to clean before they left. She was thinking of how they were planting all of listening bugs and all other kinds of other things her imagination was coming up with.

She heard the sound of shattering glass behind her, then the screaming. Before she had a chance to turn around her own window shattered and a beam of sunlight struck her in the face. It felt like fire and without thinking she dove to the floor. Panic set in as the confusion and the sunlight spread.

"Noctio," Boron screamed and raised his first. Black smoke blasted from his hand and covered the windows blocking out the sun in a hurry.

Talcen managed to look out the window just as the smoke covered the windows. He saw two people dressed in white with bright green stars on their chest running jumping into some off-road car that looked more like it was cobbled together with tape and wire. His own face burned by the rays of the sun, but barely as the black smoke blotted it out.

"God damned purists," he said as the smoke covered everything.

Nari's arm was burned black and she was whimpering in pain. Ticcen's face was equally black on the right side. Boron was burned on his face too but everything in him was concentrating on maintaining the spell. Talcen looked around and several others were burned in various places.

"Bloodstones, if you have one eat one. It will heal you," Talcen tried to scream over the various sounds of panic.

He reached in his bag and pulled a stone out, handed it to Boron. "Take it," he said, knowing full well that if the spell failed, they could all get fried. Boron used his open hand. Grabbed the stone and quickly and bit into it. The pseudo blood in the stone began to heal his burns. The second he seemed to be on the mend he rushed to his sister who was still doing her best to not scream out in pain. "I got you," he said and handed her another bloodstone and she took it.

"Thanks," she said weakly, bit into it.

Talcen wasn't sure how his eyes weren't burned out completely. They did sting and he didn't like it. He was going to help Nari, but she had already taken care of herself with her own stone.

"Guys. This spell. I can't hold it up forever. Just a few more minutes. I need everyone near a broken window to find something to block the light," he said and once people began to put their bags into the windows to block out the light the best they could. It only took a few seconds to accomplish. "Okay, I think we got it," Talcen said and finally closed his eyes due to the burning pain he was being tormented with. Boron let the spell go and the smoke disappeared.

Tiny streams of light burned through the cracks but for the most part, their quick job of blocking out the light worked. Boron collapsed in his seat and the others were shaken.

"It was those damned purists," Talcen said, eyes still closed. "I saw them just before the spell took hold," he said and a low murmur broke out. "They must have followed us. I heard their attacks were on the rise," Nari said and watched as a thin ray of light had burned past her as the bus rumbled forward. "I know what I am going to do when I get done with camp," Ticcen said and her anger was growing.

"Revenge, is that want you want?" Talcen asked and was worried. She was like this, even before becoming a vampire. It was only getting worse.

"Yes," she said as her face finally healed completely. There wasn't much anyone could do or say to change her mind. Talcen was feeling better and opened his eyes. Everything was still blurry but vision was improving. "You can't kill them all," he replied and she shot a glare in his direction. "Right now, I feel like I could," she said and crossed her arms.

There was no reason for this to even happen but yet, it did. Stupid outlanders and their primitive fears. Ticcen wondered just how long this had been going on. Even before she was a vampire, she heard of them and their insanity.

"Well we might live forever but you can still die," Talcen reminded her, then he noticed the streams of light coming from the outside had disappeared. As if something had blocked them out. "Weird," he said to himself and carefully pulled a bag from the broken window. "What are you doing?" Nari asked him, but he didn't respond. He expected to be blasted by the sun and everyone else prepared to dive out of the way.

But to their surprise, the normal daylight had disappeared. The sun was still in the sky but it was now a deep red orb. The stars in the sky were visible as well. The red light would have been weird to anyone else. But Talcen could see as if it were in the middle of the night. Everything was perfect to him, the others started to take their bags out of the windows too.

"Welcome to Camp Stone tooth. We will be departing the bus in a few minutes. Please collect your belongings," a deep, almost creepy sing song voice said over the speakers and Talcen and Boron looked at one another. "Okay, that's weird," Boron said and picked up his bag carefully as if it might explode if he moved it wrong or too fast.

Ticcen almost forgot what Boron had in there. She looked at her right arm and saw that that there was a shard of black glass still stuck deep inside. She reached over and pulled it out with ease. Her pale green skin sealed shut almost instantly. "One of the many perks," she said and tossed it to the floor with the rest of the glass. It landed with a soft clink and she turned her attention to the outside. The bus took a turn and the sun moved out of view. What kind of place was this, she wondered. A few seconds later the bus came to a stop and the doors in the front slid open.

"Everyone out," the voice said and slowly the others started to file off the bus one at a time.

"This is it, the last time we have to do this," Talcen said and was excited about it. "You said it," his sister replied and stood up with the others and they started to walk down the bus aisle. "I heard this place can drive people insane," Nari said as they walked.

"I don't know you that well but, I don't think that was the thing to say right now," Talcen replied and he didn't care how hot the giantess was, stuff like that was not going to make any fast friends around here. At least with anyone who might have had some common sense.

"Insanity wouldn't be so bad sometimes," Ticcen replied to her just before it was their turn to step off. Boron got out of the bus and looked around. The air was dry, there was a light breeze too. The dirt path he was standing on only led one direction and everyone was going that way. A short way down the path was metal arch spanning the distance.

In the middle of it were rusty iron letters that spelled 'Camp Stone Tooth' it looked as if it might have been hundreds of years old. The style of lettering was one that none of them had ever seen before anywhere in the Morglands. The path beyond the gate was shrouded in trees that ended in darkness.

"Like I said. Insane," Nari said with a nervous giggle and started to talk forward. "This is place is already creepy, even for me," Ticcen replied and followed her. Talcen waited for them to get a few steps ahead, then he turned to Boron.

"Dude, now's your chance to get rid of that thing. No one's looking," he said and Boron shook his head. "When was the last time a super secret place didn't have cameras watching the front gate?" he asked him and that made sense.

Talcen didn't see anything but then again there were more ways to watch someone than just a camera. "Fine, just be careful, and if you get caught. I don't know you," he said. "Yeah, but all those invisible cameras are watching us talk, so, I'm pretty sure they catch you in the lie. Come on, we're getting left behind. Let's go," Boron said and Talcen cursed that logic. Then he just hoped they weren't listening either. They walked a little faster to catch up with the others.

The four of them had watched the others approach the darkness and stop at the barrier. The arch, from post to the other side was solid black. Nothing could be seen through it, even with their vampire vision. "I'll go," a dwarven vampire said as he stepped forward into the black and disappeared. The crowd waited.

"It's fine, come on through," his voice said through the black, but just a bit distorted by the magic portal. Then the others began to step through. "See you guys on the other side," Talcen said and stepped through the black.

It only felt like walking through a wall of static electricity for a second, then nothing.

# Chapter Six

Talcen looked around and all he could see was the dark and wooded path that twisted and turned ahead of them. Even if it wasn't official, it was clear that the camp had begun. The others came out of the black behind him. "It's like we stepped into a whole new world," Nari said as she looked around.

"Yeah it is, I like it, let's follow the rest of them so we don't get behind. I imagine there are some nasty things in these trees just waiting to take a bite out of us, come on," Ticcen replied and started to move with the others. None of them were sure what the natural predator of a vampire really was but none of them wanted to find out.

There was something heavy in the shadow filled air that was setting everyone walking down the path on edge. Nobody knew where this path was going to lead, there was even a chance that it might just stop somewhere in the woods. No one knew what lie ahead.

"How long is this path. I could grow to my giant form and run ahead, find out?" Nari suggested. "No, but that is a nice thought," Boron quickly replied. "Fine, I guess we'll keep going without knowing how long is left," she replied and Talcen rolled his eyes.

"You know, what if this is all it is. What if at the end of this path is just a big party. And all of this, the woods and the iron gate, reddish sky, is just to set the mood," he said and considered that to be the truth. What if all of this was nothing more than a big ruse.

"Then, well, if it's a big party. I can't wait. But I doubt it. I wish you were right," Ticcen said and looked into the trees. She thought she someone was standing there in the dark. Watching them, she quickly narrowed her eyes to get a better look only to discover that it was nothing more than a twisted log.

"Stupid trees," she muttered to herself and looked forward again. Imagination in a place like this could be a nightmare.

Then there was a sign in the distance hanging on a post for everyone to read. 'You're almost there, don't give up now,' it read. No indication of distance or anything like that. Just a simple, old note that literally could have meant any amount of distance for a vampire. "Well, I'm glad that clears everything up," Talcen said as he read it. He wasn't all that interested in signs.

"I'm sure we won't be on this road for very much longer," Nari said and sounded like she was sure of it. "How do you know?" Boron asked her. "Because the people in front of us are disappearing," she said and stopped. They were at the back of the line and once they looked farther ahead than the next few steps.

The others were slowly fading away and didn't even seem to realize it. They all just walked forward into the void. The path continued into the endless distance, but the travelers were fading into nothing.

"Well, that's a thing," Ticcen said and slowed down. "No one else is aware of it, how come we can see it?" Nari asked as she was wondering the same thing they all were. "I have no- "Boron stopped. Yes, he did know why they could see it but it wasn't something he wanted to say.

"It must be another static teleportation spell, I'm sure it's safe," changed in the middle of talking and nodded. "I know a little magic, elf after all, I guess we can see it due to your proximity to me," Boron said with pride. "Oh, that makes no sense but hey, I'll go with it," Nari replied.

"Let's go," Boron said and increased his speed, the others did the same to catch up. The four of them walked into the void and watched themselves slowly fade away with each step. "This is so weird," Talcen said as his body disappeared into nothing.

The four of them reappeared somewhere else. The small crowd was standing in front of a stage. Twin pillars with green fire on top of each of them were on both ends. There was no one standing on the black, almost too basic looking stage for an event like this. The four of them walked forward and joined the crowd.

"What do you think is going to happen?" Talcen asked and he started to get nervous about all off this now that it was real.

"Who knows, why don't you just chill out and watch?" Ticcen asked in response. "I will, I mean, sure," he replied and tried to keep calm about the whole thing. It wasn't easy. Boron was constantly looking to the left and the right with his eyes. Expecting at any second armed guards to come take him away, but it wasn't happening.

He almost felt relief when a large hand fell on his shoulder. He yelped and jumped but it held him down tight.

"I know you're scared, Elf, but try not to be so jumpy. You're embarrassing the other half of your existence," Nari said to him and Boron was relieved it was only her and not anyone else. "I can't help it. I'm really trying here okay," he said and tried not to be too defensive. She just smiled and removed her hand.

The green flames exploded with intense energy and a deep red bolt of energy struck the middle of the stage with a crack of loud thunder. Everyone looked away for a few seconds. "Greetings Neophytes. I am Master of Stone Tooth. My name is Izor," he said. The vampire was dressed in a black suit, he was very old, the color of his eyes burned blue and his hair was jet black and shiny. He was once a human, that much was easy to tell.

"All of you are here to receive Xy's Blessing. I get that, however, nothing worth having comes easy. There are only two rules here at Stone Tooth. Rule number one, if you die, you lose your chance at the blessing. Dying includes being staked or dismantled to the point of no longer being able to continue on, you lose," he said and the crowd started to murmur.

"Permanent death, due to the decree of the new king, is not permitted here anymore. All of the traps have been modified to not include fire, beheading, or magical draining elements to comply. All of the traps we could find anyway," Izor said with a chuckle. "So, do be careful. If you find an old one and obliterate yourself, there is nothing anyone can do about it," he said and the smile never left.

"Now, all you have to do is form groups of five and make it around Lake Stone tooth. All five of you. There will be challenges. There will be traps as I mentioned and horrible beasts the likes you've never seen. The distance to get back here is twenty five miles one way," Izor said and pointed to the right. There was the finish line.

"For those of you who think you are the clever types that plan on trying to make it across the lake, there is a nasty surprise waiting for you if think about risking it," he said.

"All magic is under a level two is allowed the rest is blocked. All you get to bring is the stuff you brought with you. There are supplies on, and off the trail in red bags. Some are hidden, others are not. Some will provide advantages. Others will only give pain. Choose carefully," Izor said and smiled.

"Choose your groups carefully as well Even if you work together, you still might lose, but your chances of success go up if you can manage, after all Vampires must learn to work together. Good luck, oh, by the way. It's not a race. No one gets anything special for finishing first," Izor added and disappeared in the same red flash of light.

This time the stage went with him. To their left an arch of bright yellow and black flames appeared over the beginning of the trail marking the beginning.

"Do we stick together or do we look for new people to group up with?" Talcen asked and looked around. "If you don't mind I think at least the three of us should stick together," Boron said and looked at them. Ticcen crossed her arms.

"Fine, I guess I'll stay," she said and looked at Nari who was looking around nervously. She was the only one of the giant race here, and they weren't all that popular.

"What are you worried about, Giant. You can stick with us. Elf, Giant and two Trolls. What could go wrong?" Talcen asked them and no one wanted to answer that question. "Well, we still need one more in our group," Nari said and felt good that they didn't cast her out. She didn't realize it but Boron couldn't have imagined doing that, and if his friends couldn't handle her. He would have stuck by her side anyway.

The four of them didn't know anyone else here. They scanned the area looking for anyone who seemed to be unprepared to be in a group. Someone who was likely not expecting it. None of them were because grouping up was something new. "See anyone?" Ticcen asked, she didn't as she looked. "Nope," Boron added. None of them were sure what would happen if they didn't have five members in the group. None of them wanted to chance it, however.

There she was. Standing to the far side. Nervous, alone and perfect. A human vampire girl that was rapidly looking around at everyone.

"I got this," Talcen said and started walking towards her. "Oh, this should be good," Ticcen said to herself. Talcen quickly moved through the thinning crowd and made it to her in a hurry. "Hey, it looks like you're having trouble," he said to her.

"I, um. No. I'm fine," she said and looked away. Talcen sighed. "Listen. I'm Talcen. We're one member short of our group. You can join us. It's cool. We're a little weird but, come on. We could be friends," he said and looked around. There weren't many people that were coming in their direction, no one actually.

"I'm Amanda. Nice to meet you Talcen," she said and looked around again. Amanda was about five feet six inches tall, her skin used to be dark. Now it was a pale version of that. She had the same red eyes all vampires did at this age. Her hair was red, too.

"Come on Amanda. Let's get out of here," Talcen said and lifted his arm, outstretched his hand. He tried to smile as best he could. Amanda didn't see any other options. "Fine," she said with a slight groan. He smiled. "Hey, twenty five miles of teamwork and then we never have to see one another again. It won't be so bad," he said to her.

"Yeah, everyone used to say that, come on," she replied and Talcen nodded. "I suppose everyone does," he said, turned and started walking back to the group. Amanda followed him back to the crowd.

The others were waiting in a semi circle, talking about something Talcen couldn't hear, he supposed it didn't matter anyway. "Hey guys, she agreed to come with us," he said and they stopped talking about whatever they were talking about.

"Hi," Boron said with the best smile he could. Nari just gave a small wave. "Welcome to our group. I'm this idiot's sister. Ticcen. That's Nari, a girl we met on the bus here. Boron is the elf over there," she said.

Amanda looked at all of them. "Hi. I'm Amanda. I didn't think we'd need a group and I really don't have many, any, friends. Thanks for taking me along," she said to them.

"Hey, no problem, we'd better get started then, right? The sooner we go, the sooner we get done," Boron said to them and there was a pause, they couldn't argue with that logic. It looked as if everyone had found their groups. There wasn't anyone left, whoever organized all of this did their math perfectly.

"Through the burning archway, we go," Talcen said and just then everyone noticed a group of five human vampire, all guys, venturing forward. They looked pretty confident as they moved. Everyone watched to see if it was safe, someone had to go first.

The five of them walked to the burning arch and the second they stepped into it. Tendrils of green electricity came from all directions, it wrapped around their limbs in seconds. The five of them were dropped to the ground and the energy retracted itself just as fast.

"Okay, the arch is a trap," Boron said and nodded. "Hmm. Good thing we didn't go first," Nari said and started to walk forward. The others followed her. The rest of the groups started to walk around the burning structure carefully and nothing happened to them.

"They have the right idea," Boron said and continued. "Anyone could tell those are weak flames of entrapment, come on," he said nervously and laughed.

"If you knew it. Why didn't you say anything, why didn't anyone else?" Ticcen asked and Boron nodded. "It was fun to watch the arrogant ones get zapped, they'll be fine in a couple of hours. From now on I'll do my best to warn you guys in the future," he said and smiled.

"You better," Ticcen replied and the five them walked around the burning archway, careful not to get to close.

# Chapter Seven

The five of them walked along the path. It was weird, so many groups had started out at the same time, but it was only a few minutes into the journey when they discovered that they were alone. "This place is creepier by the second," Amanda said, holding her brown bag tight in her left hand. "Yeah, but there is something I need to do once I get the chance," Boron said as they walked.

"What's that?" Nari asked him and he sighed. "I just have to keep a promise. I always said when I got to Stone tooth, I would bring home some of the lake water," he said, making stuff up on the fly. He had no idea what he was talking about. "Speaking of lakes, don't you think we should have seen it by now? I mean this thing is supposed to be huge right. Where is it?" Ticcen asked looking around.

She expected to see it by now.

"No idea. Maybe we're just not close to it," Talcen suggested to them. There was sure to be a lake close by because all the trees, despite all of this strange magic in the air around them. There were even sounds of birds and other things here, too. It was all natural besides the reddish tint in the sky blocking out the light of the sun.

"Come on, I'm sure we'll see it pretty soon. All we need to do is keep going. What bothers me is where did the rest of the groups go. Why are we alone?" Nari asked. It was something that none of them really noticed before she said anything.

"Yeah, okay. That is kind of weird," Ticcen said and looked around. "Maybe it's like it was coming here. The weird staticportation thing," Talcen suggested but no one knew. One minute they were all together, the next, it was as if everyone found a different path, even if there was only one to take. "Who cares where they went. All we need to worry about is one another and that's it. If you want to worry about them go ahead. Me, all I'm worried about is you, not them," Boron said a little too forcefully.

Nari looked at him. "You almost sounded like you cared about us, that's sweet," she said and was a little impressed. "I do," he replied and smiled but didn't want to look at here. Sometimes you could make a woman feel weirded out if you looked too much so he as being careful not to do it.

"Boron the elf, our hero," Ticcen said and laughed about it. "The most heroic hero that's ever heroed in the history of the world. That's our guy," Talcen said as they turned a corner. Then they all stopped. Here in front of them was the lake they had just wondered about.

The water reflected the light and looked like it was blood and there was not a wave to be seen, it looked as if someone had painted it. The path continued a little to the left to lead to some kind of scenic lookout. The fence surrounding the edge was weathered and cracked.

Talcen thoughtlessly walked forward and touched it without thinking. It looked like wood but it had long since turned to stone. A hand reached forward and pulled him back. "Dude what in the hell are you thinking. There are traps, remember. If this doesn't have 'I am a trap' on it, I don't know what does," Boron said to him, alarmed. Talcen silently cursed himself and his stupid brain. "Sorry. I'll be more careful next time," he replied. "but nothing happened," he finished trying to justify what he did.

"Tal has a point. Nothing happened. I think this isn't a trap. It's just evidence that this place used to be something else once," Ticcen suggested. "Well, okay. Maybe this one time it will be okay to get a closer look," Boron said and carefully started to inch his way forward on to the outcrop. He expected it to fall, explode or something else. But nothing happened, the rest of them moved forward on to it as well.

"So, this is the lake, I wonder if it even has a name?" Nari asked. "Who knows. The outside is filled with places few people have ever seen. This fence feels like it's made out of stone. This place is far older than anyone realizes," Ticcen replied and she looked at the lake. The other side of it was only a barely visible thin black line in the far distance.

She wondered if someone was looking back at her right now, neither of them would ever know. The water looked like it was shining, but the shoreline was black and shiny. As if it wasn't sand but something else, something almost alive maybe.

"Okay, so it's a creepy lake. Can we go now?" Amanda asked, looking at the lake. It looked like every other one she had ever seen. "Yeah, this is fun and all but we should go," Ticcen agreed with her. None of them here came to just look at a lake. Talcen and Nari agreed, turned and started to walk back towards the trail. Amanda followed them along with Ticcen. Boron waited just a few seconds for them to walk a few steps away.

"Alright, now's my chance," he said to himself. He set his bag down on the ground and opened it. Right where he put it as the glowing purple crystal that was in the Grave hound.

"Okay, you're out of my hair forever," Boron said as he picked it up and threw it as hard as he could into the distance. He watched the small glowing crystal fly through the air a good distance over the lake. The thing hardly even made a splash as it hit and sank under the waves, disappearing from view. "Good," he said, zipped up his bag, picked it up and walked back to the others who were just beginning to wonder what was keeping him.

"Don't worry, I'm coming," Boron said as he hefted the bag over his shoulder. "Well good, I don't think we should get separated," Nari replied as he caught up. "Yeah, for more than one reason, come on, let's go," Talcen said as he rolled his eyes. The continued together down the path and had no idea what was going to on it. So far it seemed pretty simple.

Ten minutes past and the path hadn't changed in the slightest. Actually, it felt like they were walking in place, even the trees looked the same after a little while. Then there was something there in the distance, a figure that was tied to a stake. A stake that at the bottom of it was stacked high with firewood.

"Hey, hey you, you need to let me out of here," the person screamed at them and started to struggle.

The five of them didn't quite know what to think when they saw this. On one hand this was something they didn't expect to see. On the other, there were supposed to be all kinds of traps and this could have easily been one of them and they started to walk forward carefully.

"They'll be back at any minute, you've got to let me out," he cried again. It was a vampire, but not one any of them remembered seeing in the crowd. However, none of them looked that close at the others. "He wasn't on my bus," Amanda said.

"Not ours either," Nari added as they stopped.

"I don't know how but those purists are here. They attacked my group and we scattered. They used a sunstone. I was blinded and tripped on something. They are going to burn me. You got to let me out, they'll be back any minute," he started to say again in a panic, struggling against the ropes.

"Don't worry, I'll get you out," Ticcen said and started to walk behind him. "Tic, wait a minute, this isn't right," Talcen stopped her. "Even a weakened vampire should be able to break those ropes, any real purists would have torched him right away. Why would they leave him in the middle of the road like this?" he asked her.

"Doesn't matter. If they really are out here somewhere we can't let them do this. I don't know why they do things like this," she said. The memory of their attack hadn't faded away at all. Boron narrowed his eyes at the victim. None of this felt right to him, either. "No, maybe we should just keep walking," Boron suggested and Ticcen couldn't believe what she was hearing from them.

"Guys come on, you've got to let me out. Just undo the ropes, that's all you need to do," the man said to them, increasingly desperate to escape. "My name is Nargon, I was on the first bus. I'm from the village of Kelon, come on, hurry up. I need to find my group. They could be tied up just like me," he said, pleading with them.

"Fine. I'll leave it up to you. I just don't feel right about all this," Talcen said and Amanda stepped up. "Are you all insane? This is clearly a trap. No fanatic would have just left him unattended like this. They would have torched any vampire they got their hands on right away. Especially after going through all the effort of setting all of this up," she said and couldn't believe what was about to happen here. "I agree with the human, this feels like an awful lot like a setup," Nari said and didn't want to get too close.

Ticcen didn't understand their logic, nor did she understand the others. There were any number of reasons the maniacs left him here. She ignored them all and walked behind the stake. The ropes were tied and there didn't seem to be anything special about them. She walked forward and started to push the wood out of the way. The second she touched it, it was immediately obvious that something was terribly wrong.

The wood wasn't solid. She touched it and it caved in as if it were nothing more than clay. "What in the hell?" she asked and jumped back in a hurry. "I am Nargon," he said, but this time it was in a very different, deeper voice than before. The whole form began to change at once. The wood, the body, everything began to melt into one another.

"Run Tic!" Talcen yelled as they all backed off from the twisting form. She wasted no time and tried to run around the thing before a black tentacle struck from the increasing mess and wrapped around her ankle. "Damn it," she cried out and tried to pull away but this grip was all but unbreakable.

"Silly little undead snacks," the deep voice said and Nargon revealed itself. "Oh, come on, it's a Slime King. I've read about these," Boron said as his memory kicked in. "So, have I, they eat dead things, basically scavengers. Nothing around here is dead besides us," Amanda said and backed off further.

"It has my sister we have to do something," Talcen said, but he wasn't sure what to do. He was relatively sure that she wasn't going to be wiped out here, but there were worse things than losing your essence he supposed. "Fire, we need something to burn it with," Nari said, it was helpful, but Talcen didn't have anything to start a fire with. He expected to get supplies before this started. Every camp was that way and now he felt stupid for not paying attention or planning ahead that well.

"Boron, do you have anything?" Talcen asked just as the large, amorphous thing lifted Ticcen off the ground high above it. Under her the body turned into nothing more than a large black maw. "Ignax!" Boron shouted and pointed his left palm in the direction of the Slime King. A thin stream of fire shot out from his palm and struck the slimy beast in the side.

It screeched in pain and threw Ticcen over their heads with ease. Talcen turned and ran towards her sister while the others watched Nargon slither into the trees and disappear towards the lake.

Boron's stream of fire only lasted a few seconds. He lowered his hand but didn't take his eyes off the creature. He knew that it would come back. In a normal situation a weak fire spell wouldn't have been enough to drive something like that off, but this wasn't normal.

He wondered how they got one of the Slime Kings to work for them. They were a chaotic race that usually didn't hold allegiance to anyone. "I think we're safe for now," Boron said and relaxed after he lost sight of the thing.

"Thanks," Ticcen said as she picked herself up from the dirt without help from anyone. "I just let my hate cloud my judgment," she said, almost ashamed. "Hey, don't be too hard on yourself. You risked your life for someone you didn't know, sure it turned out to be a Slime King, but next time it might not be. That's something you shouldn't lose," Nari replied. She knew that if it was her tied up, there weren't many other vampires who would have stopped to help.

Amanda nodded as Nari said that. "I think we just beat our first trap. Way to go us," she said and smiled. There was no reason to get confident now, but she couldn't help but feel that way a little bit. "Yep, we did good. Let's get out of here before and if it decides to reset itself," Talcen said as he watched Ticcen's scrapes heal themselves, making sure she wasn't poisoned or infected with anything. She looked okay to him.

"Hey, I'm alright. It was terrifying and I was almost eaten today but I'm fine," she said, walked forward and picked up her bag as she did so. "Next time I won't be concerned," Talcen replied. Sure, she was still shaken up by all of this and there were plenty of reasons to be embarrassed, but she didn't focus on all the good qualities.

"She'll be fine," Boron said to Talcen as the rest of them started to make their way down the path again. "Yeah, I suppose," he replied. Boron nodded. "Oh, that problem we had. The soul crystal. I got rid of it," he said and Talcen raised an eyebrow. "You did?" he asked and Boron nodded.

"I tossed it in the lake, Nari and Amanda didn't see anything. So, we're safe. What they don't know won't hurt them," Boron said with a smile.

"You really threw it in the lake?" Talcen asked as the two of them started walking forward again. "Yeah, why, is that a problem?" he asked. "Well, no, I'm just glad it's gone," Talcen said and was relieved. He just hoped that again, every move they made wasn't being watched. He didn't feel watched but it was impossible to know. "Me too, man. Let's get out of here," Boron said and the two of them increased their speed to catch up to the others.

The soul crystal bounced down into the murky depths of the lake. It's purple, burning light shining down on things that had not seen the light in a hundred thousand years basked in the unknown, mysterious shine for a brief moment, then that moment was gone. It fell through the watery abyss.

Boron knew magic, he knew stuff everyone else who studied it knew. He did not understand Necromancy. It was a forbidden and dangerous art, outlawed for a reason, several reasons.

It fell, rolled over ancient rocks and then it did what every discarded soul crystal of necromancy has ever done when left to its own devices. It sought out a body. A physical form. The crystal shot through the water at a blinding speed searching for anything that would be suitable for it.

# Chapter Eight

"You know. I've never heard of a village called Kelon," Nari said as they walked the path putting distance behind them and the encounter. "The Morglands are huge, there are likely a thousand places off the map. I'm willing to bet it's a real place," Talcen said and Nari just shrugged. "Could be," she said and really didn't know.

Vampires in general weren't very adept travelers, even in their homeland. Most of them never ventured twenty miles from the place they called home after coming from Stone Tooth. "When I get out of here. I'm going to try to see all of the Morglands," Amanda said and Boron just groaned in misery. "What is it?" she asked.

"You broke one of the classic scary movie rules, you expressed ambition or the desire to do something. Now you're going to die here, for sure," he replied and she was going to punch him right then and there. "Movie rules are for movies. This is not a movie so I'll be fine," she replied to him and was angry he even said that, who does stuff like that, she thought to herself.

"Well when a monster is eating your heart or something, don't blame me. Me, on the other hand. I have zero plans. Once I get out of here. I'm going to just go home and torpor for a couple of years. Maybe by then the rest of the world will calm down," Boron replied and Amanda just looked at him. "Torpor, you're just going to sleep and hope the world gets better? Better than what?" she asked him.

"Unicorn outbreaks in the Elroxian capital, some necromancer's dirty bomb terrorist plot to blame. The blade apocalypse in the north that almost ended the world if you believe the internet. It's all a disaster and I think in a couple of years all of this will pass. So yes. Sleeping through it seems like a great plan to me," he replied.

"You actually believe the blade story, that's insane. It never happened. It was just a bunch of mages causing trouble. The blade story is nothing more than a stupid tradition held by rich people. Just another excuse to have a party," Amanda replied and the two of them started to raise their voices, not paying attention to their surroundings.

"Yeah, well I've seen pictures of the destruction, that was some impressive trouble just for some mages," Boron replied, starting to get defensive about what he believed.

"Guys, shut up," Talcen said in a hurry and stopped moving. "What is it?" Boron asked, upset that he was interrupted like this. "Fire, up ahead. Look," he said and pointed. They stopped in their tracks and looked. Sure enough there was a campfire ahead of them. "Maybe it's one of the other groups," Ticcen suggested.

"Maybe, but the sun is still out. It's hardly been two hours. Why is there a fire going when there is clearly plenty of light?" Talcen asked and no one had any ideas. "Cooking," Nari said. "I bet they are cooking something," she said and that was a good idea, but if it was true that meant it wasn't one of the groups. There was no reason for a vampire to cook anything when all they needed were the bloodstones.

"Well, it's likely a trial or a trap, something. But it's in our way so I guess we'd better go check it out. I wouldn't recommend going off the path. Who knows what's out there in the trees," Boron said and they decided that it was really the only thing that could be done.

"Just, whatever you do, don't show fear, they'll smell it," Amanda said, having no idea what lay ahead. "No fear, that is a phrase that should go on a T-shirt, someday," Talcen said and agreed.

"Come on, let's go," Ticcen said and the five of them started walking towards the fire. It wasn't very far away and the closer they got they could smell the smoke of burning wood. It smelled almost acidic as they approached. Something was off about it, like everything else around here. They turned a corner and there it was.

A man sitting by a fire, holding a metal stick into it. The man was wearing an old cowboy hat and he looked like he should have come right out of an old movie. He was a human, he also didn't seem dangerous or in trouble. He pushed a burning log around with his metal rod as they came into view. "Hey there, strangers. What brings you my way?" he asked them and didn't bother looking up. It was as if he had done this routine a thousand times over.

"Walking the Stone Tooth Trail. Just passing through," Talcen replied, he wasn't the one being asked but he answered anyway. "Good, good. Say. I was wondering if one of you could help me out?" he asked and it was clear this was a test of some kind. The five of them looked at one another. "Well you talked first, troll guy. You make the call," Amanda said, glad she didn't say anything first to the old cowboy. The eyes of the others seemed to have the same answer.

"What can we help you with?" Talcen asked and relented under pressure. The cowboy adjusted his hat. "I need you to go in there and get my red bag. I lost it trying to escape," he said and pointed straight across from him. They didn't see it before but there was a cave entrance in a stone wall. "This place is warping reality around us," Boron said, he realized it now and understood why none of the groups traveled together.

"Gee, thanks for the update," Amanda said and shook her head, she was pretty sure they all understood what was going on by now.

"What were you trying to escape?" Talcen asked. He knew this was a test, but he was also sure that all the tests here were optional, at least some of them had to be. The man looked up. "Cave is infested with goblins, nasty buggers that like to steal everything they can get their hands on," he said in that same, tired voice.

"If I go in there I'll need a weapon of some kind," Talcen replied and there were a few seconds of silence. The old cowboy pulled that metal poker out of the fire and tossed it to him. Talcen caught it by the hot end and his flesh started to sizzle at once. He didn't feel the pain but quickly grabbed the other end.

As soon as he did it turned into a silver sword. He grunted in mild discomfort. Silver was something most vampires were naturally allergic too. The hilt was wrapped in leather. The whole thing looked as it if was cobbled together in shop class by some kid.

"There you go, get my bag or give me the sword back," the man said. "Guys. I'm going to get us our first red bag. I'll be back," Talcen said, took a deep breath and started walking towards the cave. "Well, if he gets eaten. I get his room," Ticcen said to herself.

"I'm not going to get eaten," he replied and started walking towards the entrance. The thought about taking a torch with him to help fend off the Goblins, but the fire was only going to make him visible to everything inside the cave immediately. He took a moment to gather his thoughts and walked inside.

He crossed into the black and his eyes adjusted to the total darkness immediately. It was like very cave he'd ever seen on television and just how he expected it to be. He listened and strained to see any evidence of any goblins anywhere, but he couldn't. All he knew about them, really, was that the liked to live in the Southern Kingdom and they kept to themselves. What they were doing all the way over here, he had no idea.

Talcen stepped farther inside and it was then he heard shuffling to his left. He froze in place. There it was, a goblin. Goblins were short, green. It was wearing rags as most of them tended to like. This one was drawing something on the wall and had no idea Talcen was even inside. All of this was very strange. It was pitch black. He assumed the goblin could see in the dark too, just like he could. He crept over to the little guy and got a better look at what he was drawing.

Talcen's eyes widened. It was an escape plan for him and the others, however many were here in the cave. He understood what they were doing here now.

They were prisoners of the cave, of this place. None of them lived here by choice.

"Hey," Talcen said and the Goblin froze, spun around and attacked. Talcen slammed his blade into the ground and grabbed the goblin, then he put his hand over the thing's mouth in a hurry. "Listen, I don't want to hurt you," he said but the goblin struggled anyway. Much like a beaten dog might struggle from being in a cage. A vampire was one of the strongest things in the living world, even a neophyte like him. "Stop fighting," Talcen said and held him down. The goblin stopped struggling after a few seconds.

"What does dead thing want, do you want to eat me?" it asked in broken words. Talcen thought about it. Blood was blood after all and it didn't matter where it came from. "No," he said in a whisper. "I came looking for a red bag," Talcen said and the goblin pushed himself away in a hurry. "Red bag is ours to protect. So many die but we always try to protect," it said and Talcen was getting the picture of what was going on here.

"I don't want to kill you or anyone else, all I want is the red bag. Can you show me where it is?" Talcen asked again and the goblin stood up, dusted off its dirty clothes. "Dead things lie, dead things kill us. You can't be trusted," it said and stared at the silver sword in absolute terror. Talcen knew these things were being slaughtered by others, the vampires were using them for something.

But something about these little creatures got to him. He didn't want to kill any of them. He actually felt sorry for them right now and couldn't believe his race would do something like this. Maybe the eradicating purists had a point after all, this was insane. "Keep the sword," Talcen said and goblin recoiled. "You are tricking me, you will bite me, drink me," he was starting to lose it.

"No, I won't. Like I said. All I want is the red bag," Talcen replied. The goblin looked at the stone ground. "Fine, fine I take you to bag, I'll trust you," he replied. And Talcen stood up straight. He towered over the Goblin but made sure not to try and seem too aggressive in the process. "Follow me, follow me," the goblin said and started to run off into the dark. Talcen didn't have to walk too fast in order to keep up with the small one.

As they moved Talcen couldn't help but notice small goblin bones scattered off the path. Just how long had they been here. How long had they been slaughtered for some kind of a stupid test like this? It was making him angry. He was just glad Ticcen didn't see it. She would have likely changed her allegiance and he wasn't going to tell her about this. Soon enough they came to the end of the cave and there hanging on a hook was a red bag.

"Take bag, leave the way you came. Don't come back," the goblin said to him in a hurry and ran off into the dark. He didn't see any other goblins, but he could hear them chattering in the distance. "Thanks," he replied, grabbed the bag. It was nearly weightless to him. Whatever was in here couldn't have been that special, he thought as he started to walk back to the entrance. It was a short walk and there was that sword sticking where he left it.

"Keep it," he said and walked past.

Talcen came out holding the bag, the cowboy had disappeared and any evidence he was even there. When he turned around the cave was gone too. The four of them were standing there, looking as if they had just seen a ghost disappear.

"All an illusion," Talcen said. "There weren't any real goblins in there. Just this red bag," he said and held it in front of him.

"Well, open it up, let's see what's inside," Amanda said and they were all wondering what it could be. Talcen pulled the string on the bag and didn't know what to expect so he backed off. There wasn't any kind of stream of light or anything magical about it. "Are we sure there Is actually something in here?" Amanda asked, she wasn't convinced getting this thing was worth it.

The others waited for something to happen, but nothing did. Talcen got frustrated, turned the bag upside down and shook it. It was only then a small piece of white paper fell out of it. "Hmm, not exactly what I was expecting," he said as it fell to the ground. Boron reached down and picked it up.

"Congratulations, group. You've obtained your first item bag from the Cave Goblins. Feel free to keep the sword you obtained from the spirit by the fire," Boron read out loud and they all looked at Talcen.

"I don't see any sword," Nari said, looking around. The others immediately knew something wasn't right. Talcen looked around and stood up. "I might have left that in the cave," he said quietly and shook his head. "It was made out of silver, it was painful to even hold. It wouldn't have done us any good," Talcen tried to defend his actions. "And what about the goblins, was it useful against them?" Boron asked him.

"Okay, there was only one goblin and it never attacked me. I didn't feel the need to kill it. I'm a vampire, not a bloodthirsty maniac," he admitted and the other four looked at him as if he was insane. "You know what I mean, guys," he said and shook his head. "I'm not going to kill something that's barely even a threat to me," he said.

"Talcen, we are vampires. Top of the food chain. I think the whole point of this experience to let all that living stuff go," Amanda said and continued. "I thought trolls were supposed to be tougher than this," she finished and walked away.

"Human has a point, you should have just eaten the thing. It could have real blood, too," Boron said and was equally disappointed in his friend's choice. "Well I think that maybe mercy, even for a vampire isn't such a bad thing," Ticcen said, defending his actions. Nari just shrugged, not knowing what to say about the issue.

"Okay, the next quest or mission I'll let you guys do it," Talcen said, he was half relieved at this, too. He was feeling like a leader by default and the last thing he wanted to do was lead this group and be responsible. "That sounds like a good thing to me. Maybe we'll get something useful next time around," Nari said, trying to put a positive spin on it, but to Talcen it just sounded like it was more anger. "Yeah, next time we might get something useful, come on let's get out of here," he replied and started walking away.

The others were upset at what he did, or more to the point didn't do, "It was a silver sword anyway, it's not like it would have helped any of us," Talcen said under his breath and in anger. No one heard him as they walked away down the path. They had no idea what was going to be in front of them or what would come up next.

# Chapter Nine

That red sun burned across the sky and time felt faster than normal here. Maybe it was, none of them had experienced a full day in so long that the speed of the sun seemed unnatural. Pretty soon it was hanging low in the sky.

"So, when do we do our next thing?" Boron asked, he as getting annoyed at all this walking they were doing. "Hey, maybe we get lucky and there isn't a next thing. Maybe all we get to do is just kind of chill out here and not worry about it. Maybe we're the last group that made it," Amanda said, she wasn't minding the easy trip, however everything looked like it was the same. There was nothing to indicate that they were going anywhere at all.

"This place has to be under a bigger spell than just to block out the sun," Nari said, she too wasn't feeling good about this whole endless walking thing. Ticcen just shook her head. All the complaining was getting on his nerves and Talcen was hoping for all the distance he could get between him and the cave. Mentally and physically, he didn't mind all the complaining at all.

"You could take a look, you know?" Boron asked Nari. "You want me to grow and look ahead?" she asked and stopped. "Yeah," he replied and the rest of them stopped too. Nari looked at him and smiled "Sure, I thought since last time I asked you'd be embarrassed if I did," she said and it was clear that if she still could.

"Nah everyone knew already, we just figured that we didn't want to show off," Talcen said and continued, "But, hey, come on. None of us will tell anyone if you do it, just once," he said and the others nodded. Nari looked at them. None of them seemed as if they were repulsed or horrified by the idea. She smiled. "Thanks, friends," she replied.

With a quick motion she pulled out the orange pendant from under her shirt and carefully unhooked it from behind her neck. "Hold this for me," she said as she took it off and tossed it to Boron. He caught it and was surprised how heavy it was, even to him.

"And stand back a little," Nari said as she took a deep breath and closed her eyes. Nari was quickly engulfed in a bright green and orange swirling fire that shot up into the sky. The four of them quickly backed away.

The fire took a humanoid shape in a hurry and Nari reappeared in the same clothes she was wearing before. But now she was standing seventy feet tall, towering over the trees. "I think I'm in love," Boron said to himself, he was pretty sure no one else actually heard him say it.

Nari looked ahead of them. The trail and the sea of trees went on for what looked like forever, however, there was a house that was around the next few corners. No doubt another trial or trap.

She didn't see anyone else walking the path. Nari looked down at her companions and felt as if she could crush them, in fact she knew she could. They trusted her and despite her sudden size, didn't run away. They must have been telling the truth. She pointed at Boron quickly and motioned for him to come closer. She didn't want to talk like this because her voice could have done major damage to them, undead or not. Boron kind of understood what he needed to do.

"Fine," he said and walked forward with the pendant and with no further instruction put the thing against the side of her boot. Immediately the orange and green fire erupted from her body once again. Boron figured he was going to be fried, but to his surprise there was no heat coming from the flames. The process reversed itself and she shrank back down to her nine-foot stature. When the fire died out he was holding the pendant against her arm.

"Thanks," she said and took it back and put it back around her neck.

"No, thank you," Boron said, trying to act completely normal. "Alright. There's an old house down the road. I didn't see anything else around, or anyone. It is almost as if the world stopped. All I saw was the lake and endless trees in both directions," she said and realized that this was far creepier that any of them could have imagined.

"This place did have a separation spell on it," Amanda said and now realized how alone they actually were in this place. "Yeah, the house looked old. The sun is going down and I don't know what comes out of the woods at night but maybe we shouldn't find out?" Nari said. Normally the dark was not something a vampire was afraid of, but none of them had ever been in a place like this before.

"That sounds like a good plan to me," Talcen agreed as he looked at the sun. He couldn't help but imagine what nightmares were just waiting to come out to introduce themselves. It wasn't something he was looking forward too.

"We should be able to make it before sundown," Nari said, "but we'll need to go, like, now," she said and the others and started to walk in that direction.

The others followed her and didn't bother questioning it. "This is going to be a death house, isn't it?" Ticcen asked them. "I would be highly disappointed if it were anything else," Amanda answered for them. Boron was really hoping it wasn't a death house, he really could have gone without another trap today.

They walked for a short distance further and sure enough there was a house there just like she said. It was weird, as if the next thing showed up only when they started to ask about it. There was no real way of knowing if this house would have been here or not if they never asked. It looked as if it had stood here forever in this wilderness. The paint was all gone and it had two floors on it at least. There was a stairway leading to the main door.

"Home sweet home, I guess," Ticcen said and was the first one to test the steps.

She put her foot on the first one carefully. The others were close enough to pull her back in case it was another trap. Nothing happened, however. "Well, I guess it's not a slime monster," she said and the others approached the house, too. The stairs looked weak but as they walked up there wasn't a single creaking sound indicating it. "You could have just thrown something at it instead of risking your whole leg," Amanda replied.

"She's got you there," Boron added. "Shut up, they wouldn't do two slime monsters twice in a row," Ticcen said but had no idea.

They got to the door and Talcen opened it. He expected it to be locked but it wasn't. To their surprise everything inside so far was in pretty good shape. This made all of them nervous. There was no reason to think all of this would stay this way. "Boron, do you feel anything here?" Talcen asked him. Boron looked around, he was trying to sense any kind of magic around. If there was any around he sure couldn't feel it.

"Nothing, it feels clean. I wouldn't rely on that. Also, I would recommend sticking together," he said as something about this place didn't feel quite right to him, even if he couldn't feel any magic around. "Stick together, yeah I can do that," Amanda said and closed the door behind them. She was worried that things outside would attack while they weren't looking.

"Where do we go first. Everything on this trail has some kind of purpose, right?" Nari asked and walked forward a little. "Well, that's the running theory. Of course, I kind of doubt that the theory means much here. This place was also made to weed out the weak and unworthy. We're not safe here," Talcen replied. He wanted that blessing more than anything right now and there was no chance that he was going to let some likely haunted house prevent him from getting it.

The last rays of light faded from the windows. Their night vision was perfect, but still there was no sign of any kind of life in the house. "Come on, we can keep moving tomorrow. Let's find a room and have a snack. I'm getting hungry," Nari said and walked toward what looked like the living room. The others followed her inside.

The living room was nice, if not strange. The carpet was red, the walls were brown. There was one sofa along the far wall and a television on the other side. "Good times, reminds me of a party I went to once," Boron said and walked in. "I don't think I want to know about any parties you've been to," Amanda replied.

Boron rolled his eyes and ignored her. "Well, I suppose if something was going to pop out and attack by now, it would have. I'm going to sit down right here on the couch and have a bite," Talcen said and did so. Everyone tensed up as he did, they expected terrible things to happen, but nothing did.

"Cool," Nari said and joined him. Ticcen sat on the other end. "I guess that just leaves the floor for us," Boron said to Amanda. "Yep, I guess so," she replied and the two of them sat down in a hurry.

They started to get bloodstones out of their bag and one by one bit into them while trying to still pay attention to their surroundings just in case everything decided to go bad in a hurry.

This place wouldn't be so bad, if only weren't an obvious death house," Ticcen said as she looked around. "Well if's it's a death house, it's being really bad at it," Amanda said as she held her blood stone in her hand.

"Maybe it's a safe house for the night, didn't anyone think of that?" Nari asked and the others considered that for a second, but no none of them believed that. Nari could tell that no one believed her. "Well, it doesn't seem dangerous right now, at least," she said mostly to herself, defeated this time.

The group carefully tried to relax in the house of mystery, it was safe enough for now, almost safe enough to relax a little.

# Chapter Ten

"Group seven made it to the house, sir," a vampire said sitting at the monitor. "Good, give them a few minutes of rest then we'll let loose the construct situation," Izor replied with a smile. He looked on the ten monitors and so far, every group had done pretty well for their first day into the trip.

All of their progress was about the same, too. Izor was pleased with this and had the next step of the trials all planned out when suddenly an alarm started to blare.

"What in the hell is that?" Izor asked and tried to find the source. It only took a few seconds before he figured out that it was coming from the lake. "I don't know, it doesn't make any sense," the vampire at the controls said and focused in on the lake.

"Is someone stupid enough to try and cross it?" Izor asked. "Give me a visual," he said and the screen flipped to a live feed. No one was crossing it. The lake was boiling in the center, well it looked like it was anyway.

"No really, what in the hell is that?" he asked again. "No idea," his assistant replied. It looked as if something was breaking loose from the bottom of the lake.

"Is there anything down there that we don't know about?" Izor asked and his blue eyes flared as the light of the screen hit them. "There are plenty of things down there we don't know about, sir," the assistant replied and Izor wondered what was going on now. What kind of thing was going to come up from the depths and ruin his whole day.

All they could do is watch the lake from here. "Should we send a team in to investigate?" the assistant asked him. "Yeah, get one in. Tell them to be ready for anything," Izor replied, but he never took his eyes off of the disturbance in the water. He wasn't comfortable about any of this.

# Chapter Eleven

The team appeared on the black shores of the lake. The sand was much more solid than it looked. "This is Alpha team arriving on the western shore, everything looks normal from here. The Disturbance in the lake is unchanged," Bill said into the radio as he and two others looked around to make their first impressions.

"That's great, could you please find out what is setting off the lake alarm and make it stop," Izor replied from the other end. "Yeah, we're on it," Bill replied and motioned for the other two to get into the water. They finished zipping up their suits and putting on their head gear. "I hate water missions, why couldn't if just be one of the goblins making a mess or something like that," the one on the left said as he made sure his weapon was ready to go. The one on the right nodded and readied his weapon, too.

The two of them walked into the black water and quickly disappeared beneath it. Bill waited for a report, it could have been anything down there. He was sure it wasn't much of a match for a couple of vampires though. Not many things in this world were. Bill waited a few minutes before getting a report in.

"What do you see?" he asked into his radio. No reply, there always was a small delay when working with water though, something about it seemed to slow down transmissions. "Nothing yet, whatever is down here is kicking up one hell of a mess. We can't see more than just a few feet in front of us," a voice replied. "Alright, keep looking and whatever it is, be careful. It could be dangerous," Bill replied and waited. He looked out to the lake and still there was a great disturbance out there that was continuous. He'd never seen anything like it.

"Bill, I can't believe what I'm seeing down here. We're coming up," the man said and Bill was confused. "Tell me what is it so I can report in," Bill replied.

More nothing, he hated the delay that the water caused, especially at times like this. There was always a delay but it never lasted this long. "Guys you're making me nervous, what is going on down there?" Bill asked again and raised his weapon in the water's direction.

Seconds later two figures broke the surface and quickly swam to the shore. "Bill, it's a damn golem. We need a golem hunter down here right now," the one on the right said and turned around, weapon trained on the water.

"Bone golem, sir. I know it's hard to believe but that's exactly what it is down there," the other one said. Bill didn't understand how one of them got down there but this wasn't a good thing.

"Izor, it's a Bone Golem. They said one is coming up to the surface. We'll need a professional down here as soon as you can get one," Bill said into his radio and they started to back away from the lake. "A golem, that's not possible. There hasn't been one of them in the Morglands in over a century," Izor replied in shocked and disbelief. "I was there when the last one was destroyed. I remember," Izor said as memories of war began to flood his mind again.

Bill didn't believe it either. It was about then the disturbance in the water stopped. "Maybe whatever powers the thing snapped back into activity?" Bill asked. It wasn't uncommon for old things to snap back to life, especially magical things like golems. Golem hunting in the outside was a common thing, but not so much inside the walls.

The water in front of them began to rise up. Seconds later the surface broke and it revealed a black, thick boned demonic looking thing with purple burning eyes. It towered over all three of them at seven feet tall. "What in the name of Xy–" Bill said and never finished it. "Fire," he said, getting his situational awareness back.

The three of them opened fire. Their red laser beams flew forward and struck the thing as it lumbered out of the lake. It didn't even notice the lasers as if they were merely laser pointers one might use to entertain the family pet. "What in the hell, turn it up to full," Bill ordered, they quickly did this as they backed off and fired again.

The three beams slammed into the thing's chest and did nothing but bounce off. "Okay, we need to retreat," Bill said in a hurry. The other two were going to activate their retraction spells when the thing leaped forward. Long silver spikes grew out of the top of its wrists and tore through the chests of the two of them at the same time.

"No!" Bill screamed and watched as his two team members crumbled into ashes at once in front of him. Then the thing tore the spikes straight up sending the ashes to the air and watched as their red essence flowed into its own body and any hope of resurrection along with them.

Bill disappeared from the lake. The black boned golem stared only a second where Bill once stood, his purple burning eyes turned to the forest. Then it walked forward into the trees and blended into the darkness without a sound.

Bill appeared at the command center, visibly shaken at what happened. "Bill, what happened, where are the others?" Izor asked, fearing he already knew. "It's a damned black bone golem. How in the hell did one of them get here?" Bill demanded to know. "I don't know. I didn't know one was down there. They didn't mention it," Izor replied and felt betrayed.

"We can't let those kids out there roam around with a monster like that. Lock this place down, now," Bill said and continued. "You need to declare an emergency until we can get a hunter on site to take care of this," Bill said and Izor nodded. "You're right, we need to do it. I'll do it right now," he said and rushed to the command center.

"Open up a channel to everyone right now," he said to the assistant as he got on the microphone and considered his words very carefully. If he turned this into a panic situation it would make everything worse. It only took a few seconds but he knew what he was going to say.

# Chapter Twelve

The five of them were still in the house. Nothing had changed for hours now and they were pretty sure that Nari was right about this being a safe house. They had finished their blood stones and without anything to do, they were all getting pretty bored. "So, does anyone have a deck of cards?" Amanda as she was staring at the celling. No one answered right away.

"From all the things I heard about this place. Sitting around and being bored wasn't one of those things anyone talked about," Talcen said and all of this nothing was starting to make him nervous. There was supposed to be something else going on, literally anything else. He was about ready to go back outside and take on anything that might be there when there was a loud click that broke their routine.

"Guys, I think we're locked inside," Nari said and looked around. Giants hated to be locked in anywhere, the very thought of this made her anxiety level go through the roof and she grabbed the pendant around her neck ready to tear it off. A hand wrapped around her own.

"Calm down, okay, we're fine," Ticcen said and looked her in the eye. Nari slowly let her pendant go and did her best to not panic, even being a vampire, some traits were impossible to break. "Okay, okay," she said and did her best to listen.

"This will be a test, I'm sure," Talcen said and waited for the next part to happen, anything at all, and it was about time. The television that didn't work earlier snapped on, but it was only static. "This is a camp wide message. We have encountered difficulties and for your safety we require everyone to stay where you are until further notice, that is all," the voice said and the five of them looked at one another.

"What do you think that could be?" Amanda asked but none of them knew. "I'll bet this is just another test. They want real vampires, not obedient little sheep that just do what their told," Ticcen said and the others considered it.

"If this is that, then we should get out of here. If the danger is real we'd be doing something really stupid," Boron said and he couldn't decide. It didn't make any sense that they would have just threw a warning out here like this just as a test, there would have been a whole better to do something like this. Boron just didn't know what to do next.

Nari was still borderline panicking. "I think we should get out of here. This could be another trap and anyone who stays here is finished," she said to them trying her best to act calm. "How are we going to decide what to do?" Ticcen asked them straight out, she hated when they wasted time. "Even if it's real, this place is so big we might never encounter it. I say we go," Amanda said, looking outside. She wanted to get this stuff done as fast as she could, there was no telling how long they were going to have to wait here for the all clear signal.

"I agree with her. Sitting around here is pointless. This place is vast and it warps reality. None of the groups are on the same path, not really. Chances are really high we never see what this emergency is," Nari agreed, almost hopeful. She hated being trapped anywhere and anything to get out of here, she was all for it.

"That sounds good to me," Boron agreed. Stay or go, either way was fine with him. Some vague emergency didn't bother him much. It couldn't have been anything that serious. Ticcen just shrugged in agreement. Talcen did the same.

"Then I guess it's decided, we're leaving," Talcen said and they all started to pack their stuff back up. It didn't take too long to gather their things. The empty husks of bloodstones slowly were slowly evaporating away in a corner.

Boron walked to the door and carefully put his hand around the door knob, sure enough it was locked. Boron drew back and thrust his right foot into it. He bounced off and took a tumble backwards. "Ouch," he said as he hit the floor. The others laughed at him and he looked away. "Well, you guys do better. I think it's locked with magic," he said with a groan as he lifted himself up.

"I just think you didn't kick it hard enough. Do better," Nari said in a huff as she walked to the door. She drew her left leg back and thrust it forward as hard as she could. This time the wooden door snapped in half and fell off its hinges. "See, that's how you do it," she said and walked outside in a hurry. The night air felt good. The others followed her out. If there was any kind of danger out here they couldn't tell. Nothing had changed.

"It feels safe to me, let's get out of here," Nari said and she started to walk down the path. "Hey, wait up. The rest of this place might still be active, you know?" Talcen said and the rest of them chased after her in a hurry, getting separated now was the one thing they didn't want to do, especially now.

# Chapter Thirteen

"Sir, we have a problem," the assistant said as he looked at the monitor. "One of the groups has decided not to listen to the lockdown," he finished and Izor whirled around to look at the screen. "Damn it, there's always at least one group that just doesn't know when to quit. Usually I would commend it but today isn't that day," he said.

"Stone tooth is a dangerous place, if they die, I guess they die. I can't say I didn't try to stop them," Izor said and walked to the phone. "Bill, do you know any good Golem hunters we can call because this is an emergency and I want to keep this quiet," he said to him and Bill thought about it. "Nope, can't say I know of and, wait actually I know one," Bill said and snapped his fingers.

"I think that Thodon would do the trick in this situation," Bill said and nodded. "I only hope he's not on some mission right now," he finished.

"Call this Thodon and see if they can help us as soon as you can," Izor said and Bill nodded as he walked over to a phone, picked it up. Bill dialed a number and put the phone up a second later. The phone only rang once. Bill had no idea what he was going to say so he decided to stick to the basics. "Hey, how's it going?" Bill asked and immediately went back on his choice to get to the point.

"Good, so are you busy right now? We have a problem up here in Stone Tooth," Bill paused. "A golem shaped problem. It has black bones and it's huge. You came to mind first," Bill said and then he smiled. "Great, I'll send you my location and see you in a few minutes," he said and hung up. Bill pushed a few buttons and sent Thodon his location.

"He'll be here in a few minutes," Bill said and put the phone in his pocket. "Thodon isn't a vampire, you should know this," Bill said and Izor was confused. "You're going to send a living being into a camp full of vampires and a killer golem. Don't you think we should keep this in the Morglands before we bring in outside help?" Izor asked him and Bill nodded.

"We don't have a choice. Any vampire that goes up against that thing is bound to be destroyed. It was made to kill us, I think," Bill said, he didn't see very much of the monster but he was pretty sure that outside help was unavoidable in this situation. Izor just nodded in response and turned to look back at the screen.

All the groups were indicated with blue dots on the screens. The golem was a red dot and it was just moving in a straight line. "At least we can track the stupid thing," he said and was happy for small favors like that.

Then there was a flash of white light and it got everyone's attention in a hurry. "So, I heard you had a golem problem, tell me everything you know," Thodon said. He was dwarf dressed in black armor and had black axe on his back, two guns on his belt and a sword crossed with the axe. He had a gruff voice and dark brown eyes.

"It's a black bone golem. We had no idea it was here," Bill said and that was about all he knew. Thodon couldn't believe it. "A vampire killer, here, that doesn't make any sense at all," Thodon said and thought about it. "Nope, still doesn't make any sense. What else do you know?" he asked and Bill thought about it a little more.

"It has purple eyes they are burning, like fire is coming out of its head," he said and that was all he really knew.

"It looks like a Necromancer has broken into camp, purple fire is one of their trademarks and mostly used in reanimation magic. It takes a powerful necromancer to conjure that up. I figured you would have detected one of those long before they ever got in here," Thodon said and was confused.

"No, no god damned Necromancer got in here. We would have seen it. We would have noticed that," Izor shot back in a hurry. The mere thought that a monster like that could get in here was insane, yet all the evidence pointed to just that. A high leveled necromancer lurking somewhere in Stone Tooth.

"Listen, it doesn't matter. I'll do my best to kill this Golem, however, my fee is this. First. I keep anything it has on it. Weapons, precious metals or anything else. Second, one hundred pounds of gold delivered to my account upon completion of the task. This kind of golem hasn't been seen in over a century, who knows what kinds of tricks it has. This will be especially dangerous," Thodon said and Izor was stunned, the first part was no problem. "One hundred pounds of gold, I don't know if the king will agree to that," Izor replied and Thodon nodded.

"Alright then, I'll be on my way. Good luck with your golem problem," he said and started to reactivate his teleportation rune.

"No, wait. Don't worry, we'll get your gold. No worries. You kill the golem and you will be paid, I promise," Bill said and he didn't know how he was going to get that much gold but he needed to figure it out. Thodon looked to Bill. "Good man. I'll see you when it's done," he said and looked at the screen. "Oh, come on, I would have thought you locked the place down why is there a group still moving around out there?" Thodon said and noticed that the blue and the red were going to meet very soon.

"We tried but you know how some people are, they refuse to listen," Izor said and hated the fact that he had to say it. But there it was, the cold fact of the matter. "Fine, whatever. Give me the location on this layer and I'll go there to try make sure none of them die," Thodon said, he wasn't sure he could save anyone but he'd give it his best shot. "Level B-2," Izor replied. Thodon activated his teleportation rune and disappeared in a flash of white light.

# Chapter Fourteen

The darkness seemed thicker as they walked down the path. It had always been quiet before. "Do you think there will be any more traps. I'm starting to think this place is more theme park than say, you know, intense trail," Amanda asked and the others weren't sure. "Oh, you know how it is. Whatever the emergency is, it's got them all shut down," Boron said with a smile.

"We're going to be done with this in no time at all at this rate. I was sure that there was going to be more to it," Nari said, she didn't care if there were traps or not. She was just very happy to not be trapped like a rat in someone else's cage. "I can almost taste that blood now," Talcen said with a great smile.

"Yeah, me too," Ticcen said and they kept walking through the dark and the moonlight when suddenly there was a heavy and loud snapping sound. In the distance. "What in the hell is that?" Amanda asked and Boron snapped his eyes in that direction. He couldn't see anything through the trees. "Sounded pretty big whatever it was," Ticcen suggested and the others agreed with that. It could have literally been anything and right now they were not ready for it.

"This would have been so much better if we had a weapon or something," Boron said and was bitter. "Again, sorry about all of that, but we aren't defenseless," Talcen replied and wasn't sure what to do. Then the snapping sound came again, closer this time. "What the hell, does anyone see anything?" Boron asked and the fact that he couldn't was making him feel very uncomfortable about all of this.

"Guys, why don't we just run?" Amanda asked them. All of this was getting to be too much. Too intense for her and she wasn't used to it. This must have been how movie characters felt. "Yes, your right, let's get out of here, it's stupid to stay," Ticcen agreed and the five of them started to run down the path, away from whatever was making the horrible noise behind them.

There was a great chance that something just as bad waited for them down the path and they would run directly into it, but it was a chance they were willing to take right now.

After a few seconds of running the noise behind them was gone, or at least too far away to be heard. "Okay, stop," Amanda said and the five of them did. None of them were out of breath but Vampires had a very limited amount of energy. Bloodstones provided just enough to get by and exist but it was nothing compared to the real thing.

"What do you think it was?" Boron asked as he stared down the dark path behind them. He couldn't see anything approaching them at all.

"Something dangerous, big, you know. Standard monster stuff," Ticcen replied. "Wow, you're not helpful at all," Talcen said and Nari shook her head. "You know, I don't know why we were running. I could have taken it. Whatever it was I highly doubt it was bigger than I am," Nari said and everyone wondered the same thing now that they thought about it. It seemed silly to be so afraid right now.

"Well, okay. If it shows up again we'll just give it a giant sized kick in the face," Amanda said and turned to look down the path. "Construct," she yelled and backed up. The others turned to look and it was not just one, but several of them wandering in their direction. The humanoid figures were in various states of decay as they moved forward.

"This is something we can handle, they aren't any threat to us," Talcen said and shrugged. He was pretty sure Amanda was, for whatever reason, scared of these things. Being a human once, it only made sense. Humans called them zombies and were often afraid of them. "It's alright Amanda, we'll handle them for you. You can get the next one," Talcen said and Amanda backed off a little more. She stared into their dead eyes and couldn't help but be afraid of them.

The other four prepared to dispatch of the lumbering constructs out when a heavy, large thing fell out of the sky in the middle of the pack. The impact did not cause the constructs to fall over but the wave of white fire that erupted in all directions from the thing did. The feeble things fell to the ground. Whatever kind of fire this was, it kept them down where they fell. The vampires were just out of range of the radius and backed off when they saw it all at once.

Boron noticed the purple burning eyes first. "Purple eyes," he said in disbelief. "This isn't, that's not possible," he said mostly to himself. "Oh, hell, I was right," Talcen said out loud. His story of the Golem under the lake, he just read that on an urban legend website. There was no way it could have been real.

"Purple eyes, we need to run, now," Boron screamed and started to run the way they came. The others followed him. Nari and Amanda had no idea what purple eyes meant besides the obvious that they could see them. "I'll explain later, let's go," Ticcen said to them as she ran past. Nari was getting sick of running away but the silver fire had changed everything.

"Damn it," she said to herself and followed them but was too slow. The black behemoth leaped forward and grabbed her by the back of the neck and effortlessly picked her up of the ground. "No!" Nari screamed as the thing lifted her off the ground, it was enough to make the others turn around.

"Boron, do something," Amanda screamed at him. Boron wasn't sure what he could do but he would give it a try. "Olek," Boron yelled as he out stretched his hand and a bright blue, but thin bolt of electricity flew from his hand and struck the black bones of the monster they faced. The blue beam spread over the golem and sent sparks in all directions at once, but it didn't let go. "If we could use stronger magic I might have a chance," Boron said, defeated.

They all watched as a long silver spike came out of the top of the wrist. Nari was struggling but the thing had an iron grip around her neck. Despite being a vampire the strength was enough that she could feel the pressure. When she saw that silver spike come out, that was all she needed to see. Immediately she reached for the pendant around her neck to pull it off. One second before she managed to do it, she hit the ground unexpectedly. "What?" she asked no one.

"If you want to live I'd suggest running," a voice said to her. She didn't bother to look at who said it, instead she pulled herself up and ran forward only a few feet before turning around. The golem was missing its right arm.

A black armored person was attacking it with a big axe. It raised its silver spike up and blocked the next attack. With one powerful thrust it sent him and the axe flying in her direction. Nari didn't want to catch him so she moved out of the way.

Thodon slammed into the ground but quickly picked himself up. "What are you still doing here. I told you to run," he said to her in an angry voice. "Where? Where should we run?" Nari asked and the two of them watched as the golem's severed arm lifted off the ground and reattached itself. "Do I look like I care.

Just get away from it," Thodon said to her and didn't expect the arm to come back to it.

"What in the world?" Thodon said to himself. Usually when golem lost limbs they didn't reattach themselves. This was new to him. Nari shrugged. "Well, alright. Have fun with the monster," she said and ran down the way the rest of the group went. Thodon watched the monster, studied it and realized something was different about it.

The regeneration thing was new but all of it, together. The whole thing was just, well, something was wrong. Thodon didn't have much time to study the golem.

The black boned thing stared at him, and even though Thodon attacked it. It didn't seem to have any interest in him. "So, a vampire killer that's really focused on its job," he said to himself. He'd only heard stories of things like this, however if he attacked it again he was sure that it was going to include him in its mission of things to kill. He was pretty sure that don't let any of the vampires die because of reasons was said at some point. He honestly wasn't paying that close attention to the details of the mission.

"Damn it," he said to himself and ran past the golem that was for now, content to move at a slow pace. As if it was sure that nothing was getting away from it now, or ever again.

# Chapter Fifteen

Thodon ran past the Golem and he quickly caught up with the others. "Hey, you guys have a serious problem, is there anything you know about this thing I should know?" Thodon asked them and the five looked at one another. "I have no idea," Talcen replied to him.

"Who are you?" Amanda asked him the obvious question here. "Thodon, professional Golem Hunter. I was called in to take care of the problem but, you know, this is a new one on me," he said and continued. "Usually Golems don't have regeneration systems so if there is anything special about you that you'd like to share, now's the time," Thodon said to them again.

There was a silence between them. Nari and Amanda began to think about it at about the same time that the three of them had something more to share and they moved together slightly. "Tell him," Talcen said then. Boron shook his head in resistance.

"Dude, tell him already," Talcen said again. Thodon stared at him, it was clear things were about to get a lot less friendly just by the way he was looking at him.

"Okay, damn it. I had a soul stone from a grave hound I found. I didn't want to get caught with it so I brought it with me and when I had the chance, I threw it into the lake to get rid of it," Boron said and Thodon shook his head and laughed.

"And here I thought there was a necromancer here. Instead it's worse, a stupid neophyte vampire played with a nightmare he didn't understand. It's coming after you because it saw all of you, but mostly because of him. He's tainted with the soul fire from that crystal," Thodon said and turned to look.

They couldn't see it yet but the thundering footsteps were still coming in their direction.

"You have to separate until I kill this thing for good," Thodon said to them. None of them really wanted to separate. "And if we don't?" Ticcen asked him. "Your chances of dying go way up. Soul fire is something that marks a target. You only get it two ways. One, if a mage puts it on you, or you handle a soul stone without protection. That thing back there thinks you're an objective for some mission. It's made to kill every undead thing it sees," Thodon explained.

Boron considered the words very carefully. "You guys. It will come after me. I need to lead it away. It will follow me anywhere. The rest of you get to the end of this," Boron said and Thodon nodded. The others shifted their eyes. Boron expected an outcry against this.

Something, anything at all. "Good luck," Nari said and took a step back. Amanda did too. She didn't know any of them and remaining alive was on the top of her things to do. Boron was about to say something but Talcen and Ticcen took a step back too.

"Guys, I'm... sorry," Boron said to them, disappointed in their choices but understanding. "I hope you live. Maybe next time when you see something laying on the ground you'll leave it alone," Ticcen said and Talcen just shrugged.

"You know how it is, man, besides. You'll be fine. You've got this guy to protect you," Talcen said and motioned to Thodon. Those footsteps were closer now and brought them back to reality. "Okay, everyone find a place to hide. Wait for the Golem to get through and then run to the exit as fast as you can. This place feels tricky so don't get lost. Go now, in the trees," Thodon said and to them and looked at Boron.

"You're with me," he said and started to walk forward past Boron. The five of them took one last look at one another then four of them dived into the trees off the path. The purple burning orbs were visible in the distance.

"Do you think it saw the others?" Boron asked. "I know it saw the others, but with them out of sight it's going to come after us, run" Thodon said and the two of them turned and did just that. The second the two of them started to run the Golem did the same thing. Thodon figured this was going to happen.

What he didn't expect was how fast it was. It was as if the thing turned into a black blur and shot down the path. Thodon shoved Boron to the side into the trees seconds before the golem reached them, slammed its black fist into the ground.

"God damn it, what are you?" he asked. Again, this thing was defying all of his expectations of what a golem could do. Not all golems were slow, but still, one this size shouldn't have been this fast. Thodon rolled over and saw the thing going in Boron's direction, lumbering as slow as it ever had before.

Now was his chance. Thodon gripped his axe and ran forward. He swung the blade. The axe blade sunk into the back of the Golem and cleaved deep. Purple energy exploded from the damage. Thodon's worst fear came true. The golem walked forward and didn't even notice the wound in the slightest.

"Damn it, kid, run," Thodon said as it pulled itself off the blade. The energy quickly stopped as the black bone sealed up in seconds.

Boron saw what happened and didn't understand any of it. He ran through the trees, clinged to the bark and with all the agility of an elf and a vampire, normally he was uncatchable. From tree to tree he flung his body, deeper into the unknown. Away from horror and directly into possibly unlimited amount more. Behind him, however the trees behind him were snapping like toothpicks.

"Oh, come on this is insane," Boron said to himself but dared not slow down. It was about then he realized that Thodon might have somehow been behind him. He was neither a vampire nor an elf. Chances were good that he got left behind. Boron stopped and spun around to look anyway. The golem was only six steps behind him and it was moving almost as fast as he was. No time to think about it he ran straight at the thing and jumped as high as he could with as much speed as he could summon.

Boron jumped over the head of the golem, its massive hands reached up and attempted to grab Boron as he did, but they were seconds too slow. He landed on the ground and rolled away. The golem turned around but his target had already started running away but he didn't get far. Boron was scanning the forest for any signs of life. There in the distance he saw one, it could not have been anyone else.

"Incoming," Boron yelled as hard as he could. He saw the heat signature turn in his direction. Thodon heard him, he hoped. Boron thought and ran towards him.

Thodon never lost track of the golem. It was really hard to lose something that smashed through everything in its relentless attack. The sound made it even easier despite how fast they were. Then the sound changed in a hurry.

"What?" he asked himself as he pulled his two cannons off his belt in a hurry. Now everything was coming back in his direction. "Damn it, kid. Why are you coming back?" he asked himself.

Seconds later Boron came running out of the mess of trees the Golem was right behind him. "Yeah, thanks for this you stupid fang," Thodon said and fired his weapons at the same time. The golem was hit in the chest with two bright white rays of light. They blasted straight through the monster's chest and knocked it to the ground, stopping it dead in its tracks.

Boron stopped running and moved over to Thodon's side. "Is it dead?" he asked him. "No, something that was never alive can never really be dead, but you really screwed up when you threw that thing in the lake," Thodon said and he never took his weapons off the golem.

"That soul stone's energy isn't just an engine, it's become, I don't know. Like an artificial soul of sorts," he said and Boron's red eyes got big.

"Then keep shooting it until there's nothing left, what are you doing?" Boron asked the first thing that came to his mind. "Because you were kind enough to give it an artificial soul and it has a regenerating ability, I don't think I can kill it unless we find a way to kill it all in one shot I don't think I can take it down," Thodon said and sure enough the holes in the golem were already starting to close.

"Well at least we can keep it down until we think of something?" Boron said and Thodon shook his head. "Nope, there is so much you don't know about golems, and I don't think that we have enough time or gun to talk about it now. Let's get out of here until we can make a plan," Thodon said, put his guns away as he turned into the opposite direction.

"We can't out run it," Boron said and was nervous. "It'll find you no matter where you go, nothing will stop it, either. It doesn't need to hurry. It will only run if it thinks it can kill you," Thodon said and Boron felt like he was going insane, his terror was worse that it had been in a long time. There was no way he could get far enough away. "No, but I have an idea to buy us some more time," he said and Thodon's hand began to glow and he slapped the vampire's arm. The two of them vanished in a burst of white light.

# Chapter Sixteen

"Do you think Boron is okay?" Talcen asked. "I have no idea. I'm just glad that monster isn't on our trail anymore," Ticcen replied, she thought he was always annoying at best and now he almost got all of them killed. The four of them walked down the dark path, nerves still shaken about what they had just gone through.

"Those constructs we saw, that must mean the campgrounds are still active," Nari said, she wasn't sure about any of it, exactly, but it made sense to her that this was the case. "Yeah. I don't know what's going to happen now that we only have four people in our group. We might be in trouble," Amanda said in agreement. None of them considered what the results of splitting up might be but now it was the one thing on their mind now that the golem was dealt with.

They took a curve in the road and there sitting in the middle of the path was a bright red, glowing bag. "Well, that's not a trap," Nari said as they all stopped to look at it. "It might not be a trap, they said some of them wouldn't be a trap. Maybe this is one of those things," Talcen suggested but he really didn't believe that.

"What are we going to do?" Ticcen asked and they stared at it for a few seconds. "Oh, what the hell, let's open it," Talcen said and walked forward. The others didn't get any closer. For all they knew it could have been an explosive just waiting to go off or anything else. Talcen stood over it and stared at the bag for a few seconds. He reached down and picked it up. Nothing terrible happened. No explosion, no trap so far. There was something inside but what it was, for now was impossible to tell.

Talcen pulled the string and opened the bag. The string disappeared as it fell to the ground. All the sudden he was extremely nervous about reaching inside of this thing. So, he turned it upside down instead and hoped something horrible didn't fall out.

Something did fall out, something impossible. A black shotgun fell out of it with a note tied to the barrel. Talcen picked the gun up and looked at the note, pulled it off. He opened the note and began to read.

"Hey. You're not good at following directions. The golem will kill all of you. Please take this weapon for defense. It is enchanted with an endless supply of ammo, however it will not stop the golem. It will only slow it down. Get to a safe place and stay there," Talcen read out loud.

"Do either of you know how to use this thing?" Talcen asked and looked at the two of them. He had no idea. Guns to him were only things that were useful in video games. "I know how to use it," Amanda said and walked forward. She grabbed the gun and checked it over. "It's a good one," she said to herself and pumped it once. "Good to know," Talcen said and continued.

"The note says it's enchanted so we don't need to worry about bullets or anything," he said again an she rolled her eyes.

"We all heard you, you didn't read that note in your head," Nari replied to him and now he just felt silly. "Anyways, we should get moving. There isn't anything for us out here," Ticcen said and they started to move forward.

"I just hope I don't need to use this," Amanda said and held the weapon down by her side as they walked into the unknown. "They'll generate another safehouse for us when they can, I'm sure of it," Talcen replied to her. "You won't have to use it," he finished and did his best to be positive. There was no point to tell them that the monster was likely heading towards them at a relentless pace and would catch up.

Talcen was growing more frustrated with every single step he took. This was supposed to be it, The final test. The ultimate challenge before getting Xy's blessing. And what happened, Boron ruined it all because he couldn't leave well enough alone. Now they were running from some golem and everything was being handed to them.

"Pathetic," he said out loud, too loud to himself.

"What's the matter?" Ticcen asked and looked at him as they walked. "It's just, you know. I feel like this whole experience is being stolen or something," he said and couldn't help but feel as if he was losing everything one step at a time. "Well, I'm sure this camp is a wash for everyone, not just you. So, stop moping. I'll bet they bring everyone back to the beginning and start the whole thing over," she said and he shrugged. "I bet we'll be the only vampires in the history of vampires to have to do this twice," he replied and suddenly the thought of that brought him a smile.

Yes, we'll be the only vampires to ever go through this twice. How cool is that? When we tell the story, though. We'll make sure to fill it with a lot of closer calls than this," Talcen went from sad to feeling a little better about all of this.

"Yeah, we'll leave out the part where you didn't know how to use a shotgun and had to give it to me," Amanda said. Talcen wasn't sure if she was messing around or didn't want anyone to know she could use one. The more he thought about it the more he realized that they didn't know anything about her, at all.

"Hey, tell us about yourself. I bet we'll have a long time after this, and who knows we might be friends when all of this is over," Talcen asked her and Amanda tightened the grip on her weapon. "What's there to tell. I was a stupid girl walking alone late at night, next thing I know I'm knocked to the ground with a pair of fangs in my back. It nearly killed me. I woke up a week later in the isolation chamber, where they told me what happened. It's not like I wanted to be a vampire," Amanda said quickly. The story didn't feel right but it was more than they had before.

"Since we're sharing stories maybe I can give mine," Nari said, feeling left out of the conversation. "Yeah, what is your story. To be honest in the last twenty years of this beginning phase I've never seen another one you," Ticcen said and Talcen had to agree. He'd never seen a giantess vampire before. This was a first for all of them.

"I was on a date with my boyfriend at the time. We were having a great time, just got out of a movie. I forget what movie now, anyway, some jerk wouldn't leave us alone. You know the type, it was an elf anyway. Making fun of giants is pretty easy to do, I guess. But stupid, too," she said and sighed. "The elf attacked us, it must have been his plan all along. He had an illusion spell on him. When Ryon defended me, the vampire's true nature was revealed. The guy killed him in a flash, Ryon was dead before he hit the ground, then it almost killed me. Teeth to the neck. Just like in all those stupid movies the humans like to make," she said and rubbed her neck without thinking as she spoke.

"I woke up like she did, in an isolation chamber. They told me I couldn't go home again and had to relocate to the Morglands. I didn't want to but, as a vampire myself, I didn't really belong anywhere else anymore," Nari said and it was clear by the tone of her voice that she was still very sad about the whole ordeal, even all these years later there were some things that she just couldn't forgive, or forget about.

The two trolls just kind of looked at one another. Before they could say anything, however, they turned a corner and found a brick house, more like a quickly built small brick square. There was a steel door, above it in bright red, neon letters it said 'safehouse.'

"Well, I guess we found it," Amanda said and started walking towards it. "It, um, it looks too small," Nari said nervously and didn't want to go inside. "I'm sure it's bigger on the inside," Talcen said and smiled. He didn't believe that, but right now keeping everyone calm was better than just being a jerk about it, even though honesty was easier, it wasn't always appreciated.

Amanda walked to the door, grabbed the knob and pulled it open. It didn't even squeak as it opened. The lights inside were already on. "Troll boy was right, It's totally bigger in here. You're going to like it, come on in," she said and stepped inside. The others followed her inside. Nari looked around and it wasn't just bigger on the inside, it was a lot bigger. She didn't feel trapped in here at all.

Talcen closed the door did his best to quietly lock it, it worked. Nari didn't hear a thing.

"Home sweet home, I guess," Ticcen said as she looked around. Then unseen speakers came to life.

"Welcome to safehouse two, it is the best we could do under such short notice. Once the threat has passed, you will be teleported to the main area," a voice said and filled every corner of the house. It didn't sound like a live voice, more of a recording.

"Oh, well, I feel so much safer now," Talcen said and fell into a chair. He could only wonder about how Boron was doing in all of this mess. Hopefully, with any luck he wasn't dead yet. Talcen still had an urge to stake him for messing everything up like he did. None of this was supposed to be happening this way. He leaned back into his chair and crossed his arms.

"We might as well get comfortable, we're going to be here for a while," Nari said and sat down on the end of the couch. Amanda and Ticcen joined them. It was big enough so that they all had a place and plenty of room between them. "The minute you relax is the minute everything goes wrong," Amanda said and held her weapon her left hand, leaning it against the couch. "I think we're going to be okay now," Ticcen replied, but she was only trying to make herself feel better and fight off the boredom.

# Chapter Seventeen

Boron and Thodon reappeared in a desolate place. Gray mist swirled around their feet. "Where are we?" Boron asked as he looked around. "We are at the battlegrounds. Izor gave me a map and if we are going to take this thing out, here is the place possible place we have to do it," Thodon said and looked around. "Battlegrounds? This place doesn't look that violent, it looks empty," Boron said and Thodon nodded. "That's the point. The winner gets the blessing or some such nonsense," Thodon said and that made Boron begin to question everything.

"You can't be right," Boron said and Thodon laughed at him. "Only one vampire gets Xy's blessing. The rest of you get to be placed into normal vampire society," Thodon said and Boron's whole world was shattered. Everything up until this point was telling him that everyone got it. "How do you know that?" Boron asked and Thodon looked at him.

"For one, I've worked with plenty vampires and they've told stories. Sorry, kid. If you were expecting glory and fortune, you're going to have to fight for it," Thodon said and looked around. "But first you're going to need the chance to do it. We need to find a way to kill this thing in one shot. Bombs, magic traps, anything. Start looking," Thodon said to him and walked off into the mist.

The battlegrounds looked empty, but if they were a kind of an arena there should have been something horrible laying around they could have used for this event. Boron walked into the mist and it was only a few seconds when a shack came out of the dark. "I'll check in the weird and creepy place," he said and walked to the door. He opened it and it was easy. Stepping inside he didn't know what to expect. He supposed that normally there were traps and walking in a door like that was instant death. Inside were various weapons on a table. All kinds of guns, explosives and other things he didn't even recognize at all.

He walked to all the impressive looking weapons and realized how useless they actually were. "One shot kill," he said to himself and looked for anything that might be that. There it was. On the wall was what looked like to him, a rocket launcher. Boron assumed it was loaded as he walked to it and picked it up off the hooks that were holding it. "Perfect," he said to himself, turned around and walked right back out of the shack.

Finding Thodon here was easy. He was the only thing warm and alive in the whole place. Boron didn't want to run with a rocket launcher, however. So, he walked as fast as he could in his direction. It only took just a few seconds to cover the distance. Thodon didn't find any weapons. He didn't seem to be looking either. Boron thought he was being sneaky but the hunter turned to face him as soon as he got close.

"This place doesn't work for the living. Nice rocket launcher," Thodon said and looked at it. "Follow me," he said and walked away into the dark. "You know more about this place than I do and I don't think I like that," Boron said as they walked. "I know a lot more than you've ever forgotten, kid, the golem is going to be here soon. It moves fast," Thodon replied and was looking for a good place to avoid getting ambushed from behind.

"Yeah whatever, how about we wait over there?" Boron asked and pointed over to another house that seemed way out of place. "That'll work. It's relentless but stupid. It'll come right for you in a straight line. I just hope that the rocket is good enough to do the job. Oh, and don't miss," Thodon said as he walked towards the house.

"I have to shoot it?" Boron asked and Thodon nodded. He reached out and put one finger on the side of the launcher and it started to decay at his touch. "Like I said, this place only works for you, it's an enchantment. This is our best chance of killing it," he said again.

"Well. Sorry I guess. I've always hated first person shooters. I can't aim worth a damn," Boron replied and Thodon sighed.

"If you miss, you die, not just staked but die forever. This is a vampire killer and you are a vampire. Do you see how this works? Hell, you might end up dying anyway. This is just the best idea that I have that might work right now," Thodon said, but there was no indication he was being sarcastic in the slightest. Boron didn't even know how this thing worked. He was staring at it trying to figure it out.

"This end here is pointed at the monster, the other end over here goes in this direction. You aim the best you can, pull the trigger. Pray if you people do that or not. I don't know what you do," Thodon said and Boron nodded. "Got it," he said, "And thanks, for everything," Boron finished. He was truly glad to have someone like him at his side for this.

"You can buy me a drink if you live through this, we'll be even," Thodon said and kept his eyes peeled out the window for anything that was different. The monster was going to come for them in a straight line. However, there was no telling where that line would lead it. There was no reason that the thing had to come from any one direction. It could just tear through the house from the side or back, however the noise it would make would be a good warning.

The two of them waited in the quiet. Listening for any noise that might be the sound of rapid and heavy footsteps crashing in their direction. "How far away did we go from where we were?" Boron asked him. "Distance doesn't work like that here. I don't understand much about Stone tooth but all roads lead here, you know? This place is weird. The sooner I get to leave and go back to reality, the better I will feel," Thodon replied. This whole place made him nervous, actually, vampires in general always gave him a weird feeling.

"You and me both. I haven't liked this place since I got here. I'm only here because this is part of the routine," Boron replied. He didn't expect to be in a half real house holding a rocket launcher and waiting for some monster to come and kill him. There were a lot of things he imagined, but this was not one of them.

In the distance, there it was. Two burning purple orbs coming at the both of them. "Remember, take your time and fire. But don't fire too late because we'll get caught in the explosion, too. We, I, at least, want to live through this after all," Thodon said and hoped for the best. "I'll give it my best," Boron replied and took aim.

The sights, if you could call it that, was little more than a square box. Boron imagined the instruction manual of thing reading something like 'put target in box, pull trigger. Hope for the best.' Boron almost laughed at that thought but he didn't want to seem like he was losing his mind right now. Keeping his cool he waited as the thunderous footsteps got even closer to him.

"Not yet, don't shoot," Thodon said and he put his hand on Boron's shoulder to calm him down. "Too far away and it could just move," he said what felt obvious, but in a stressful situation like this, mistakes were easy to make. "Okay," Boron said and relaxed a little bit.

The golem was quickly approaching and Thodon was watching it, he had watched it as if he had watched this a thousand times before. As if there was some imaginary line indicating the point of no return. It didn't take long for the monster to cross it.

"Now," Thodon said and Boron pulled the trigger. The rocket flew forward and sure enough the golem ran right into it. The explosion sent yellow and red fire in all directions and a shockwave. The ground shook, the house shook with the explosion. Boron smiled. "We got him," he said and stood up.

"Well you hit him. but I don't know if you killed him. There really is only one way to find out, I suppose," Thodon said and sighed. This was the part of the job he hated the most. "Wait, you mean we need to go look?" he asked and Thodon nodded. "Yes. It's the only way to really be sure," he said. Thodon knew that this monster could be a lot harder to kill than it looked.

"Alright, let's go," Boron said and tossed the now useless rocket launcher to the side and started to walk towards the door. "Well look who's brave now that the monster is a mangled mess on the ground," Thodon said mostly to himself and shook his head. Of course, he'd seen this a hundred times too. Rookie hunters always got a boost of confidence just after victory. Half the time the all too dead target would end up to be the end of their lives.

Boron walked out and Thodon was close behind.

The fire was burning, but dying out pretty fast because there was very little to burn. "Did it get obliterated. I'm not seeing any pieces," Boron said as he looked for anything that might have indicated that it was actually dead. "No idea, just don't get too close until the fire goes out," Thodon said and it was a good warning, he thought. Boron stopped in his tracks and stared into the fire. "It looks like we vaporized it to me," he said, but he didn't see anything.

"Kid, have you ever seen a horror movie in your life?" Thodon asked him and pulled his two guns off his belt. "The monster never usually dies that easy. This thing has a regeneration function. Be ready to run like hell," Thodon said to him and Boron didn't feel very good about that, he took and took a couple of steps back.

The fire shifted up and the burning bones of the golem stood up. It took one more step before it collapsed again on the ground face first. Thodon was quick to take aim, but didn't fire as it fell to the ground. It was hard to tell what the situation of all this was. Was it dead, dying, was this the last action of a broken magical machine. It was impossible to tell anything anymore but right now all he could do was watch and wait for the fire to go out. Only then he would know for sure.

"I always heard stories when I was a kid about the wars and how Golems were made. Millions of different kinds for the last war. I never dreamed that I would actually see one in person," Boron said, his mind drifting down memory lane.

"Kid, shut up. The minute you get distracted is the minute you die," Thodon said to him in a hurry. Boron shook his head and felt as if the hunter was just trying to get him to shut up. He wasn't very friendly about anything so far but then again this was an intense situation. At any minute they might have to run.

The fire died out and the black bones lay there, its eyes were empty and all signs of life were gone. "Is it dead?" Boron asked and Thodon had no idea. "It looks dead, but really there is only one way to tell, I suppose," he replied and took a step back. He pulled the trigger on his cannon and the beam flew into the arm of the golem. The blast knocked the thing over on his back and there was no reaction. "It must be dead," Thodon suggested and shrugged.

"Oh, that's good. Now we can get back to normal around here, finally," Boron said and stared at the thing. It was the first golem he'd ever seen and he was hoping it was the last one.

Thodon had never seen a monster like this either, a lot of it didn't make sense. How in the world did something like exist, there were too many questions he had about this whole situation he was in. Likely there would never be any answers. "I guess you can port back to your friends, I'll finish up here and take this thing apart," Thodon said and couldn't wait to see what this thing was made out of.

"Alright, I will," Boron agreed. He couldn't wait to get back and tell them he got to shoot something with a rocket launcher. How many people ever got to do that, anyway, he thought, turned around and started to walk away. "Maybe things will be looking up after all," he said and smiled.

The golem's eyes exploded with purple fire and it turned it over on its side. Its right arm thrust forward faster than either of them could react. A long silver spike exploded from the top of its wrist and impaled Boron straight through the chest. The elf vampire simply stood there as his body crumbled away into dust and his red essence flowed into the black bones of the thing.

"No!" Thodon yelled but it was clearly too late. The golem brought itself to his feet and stared at the ashes of the vampire. The golem then looked at him.

Its eyes studying him, scanning to see if he was a vampire or not. Thodon was ready to move at a moment's notice but right now he waited.

To his relief the golem turned and started to walk away. "Damn it," he said to himself and picked up the radio. "The golem killed the targeted vampire. We thought it was dead but, I don't know, I think it just played dead or something," he said into the radio.

"You what, you, how could you let a stupid machine trick you?" Izor's voice came back. Thodon rolled his eyes. "I've never seen anything like this before, usually when you take these things down they lose their energy and don't ever get back up. It's going to make a straight line to the vampires and kill them all. I have another plan. Give me the location of his friends, now," Thodon demanded.

There was silence on the other end of the radio for a few seconds. "Come on answer me, this is going to be a massacre. You need to disable your magic wards, too. This is going to be much harder than I thought," Thodon said again. "Okay, okay. I'll see what I can do about that. Anyway, they are at the red shore lake house, teleport there and beat that thing. Do everything you can," Izor replied.

Thodon hit it with a rocket, cut its arm off and shot it at near point blank range. He wasn't sure what else he could do to it. "Alright. I'll do my best, you may need to do an evacuation so get ready for that," Thodon said.

"Will do," Izor replied with a shakier voice. Thodon knew that the legacy of this place was not known for ever quitting. This might be the first time they might need to give up. This golem was never going to stop, that much was clear. Thodon pressed his teleportation rune and disappeared in a white flash of light.

# Chapter Eighteen

The four of them were just wasting time ate the cabin. Everything was looking up, at least they hoped so. "So, what does anyone want to talk about?" Nari asked, sick of the silence already. "Nothing. I just want this to end. Meet up with Boron, punch him really hard, then start this whole thing over. That's all I want to do," Talcen said in a huff.

His emotions were going between angry and proud to be the only ones to complete it twice. He couldn't decide.

"I'm sure you'll get your chance pretty soon, don't get worked up," Ticcen replied to him, she was getting embarrassed at her brother's lack of self control in this this situation. The others were doing just fine. "Hey, once we get out of here you'll have centuries to get over it. This camping trip will just be a tiny drop in a giant river of time," Amanda said to him. She was thinking of the bigger picture the vast lifespan that was being offered if she wasn't stupid about it.

Talcen could only focus on right now and wasn't quite sure why. He was always this way when something was bugging him he just couldn't let it go. "I guess you're right," he replied to both of them and needed a distraction. Something to do, anything. He looked at Nari and was going to ask a question when suddenly someone started pounding at the door, all of them jumped.

"Should we answer it?" Nari asked quietly. "Yeah. I think we should. Maybe it's Boron coming to tell us that everything is safe now," Talcen said and stood up. "It could be anyone," Amanda said and stood up. "You open the door and I'll cover you just in case it's a seven foot monster," she said as she walked to the side of the door and took aim.

"Thanks," Talcen said and walked to the door. He put his hand on the knob and pulled it open.

Thodon was standing there and Talcen relaxed a little. "Oh, it's you," he said almost disappointed. Thodon was about to talk and Talcen kept going. "So, where is Boron?" he asked and Thodon looked away.

"I'm sorry," he said and continued. "Your friend didn't make it, the golem killed him," he said and Talcen didn't believe it. "No way, he put you up to this, right?" Talcen asked, not believing it for a second and pushed his way past him outside. "Boron, where are you?" he yelled into the night, but there was no response.

Talcen couldn't believe that Boron was dead, he was upset with the elf but not that upset to wish him dead. He looked back at Thodon who's expression hadn't changed. "I'm telling you, he's dead. The monster got him. There was nothing anyone could do," he said and the others believed him. Talcen was the one with the strongest connection to Boron and the news, the reality, hit him like a powerful force, it dropped him to his knees at once.

"You were supposed to save him," Talcen said quietly, mostly to himself. "Kid, I tried but. The golem is more advanced than I thought," Thodon said and continued. "It's going to come after all of you. We can either stay here or run. Or we can fight, I have a plan if you're willing," Thodon said to them and the others didn't quite know what to do or say.

"Why don't we do both? We can get out of here and find a better place to make a stand. There has to be better places than this," Amanda said and Nari thought that was a good idea, too.

"Where would we go that's better?" Ticcen asked. She didn't know this place, none of them did. Thodon nodded. "That's a good idea," he agreed. "Let me find a place, you guys be ready to go and make sure you make sure he's ready to go," Thodon said and walked a couple steps away. The others moved to Talcen who was still in shock.

"Bro, I know this sucks but we need to pull ourselves together. We are all going to die and I'm not going to leave you here," Ticcen said to him and Talcen just shook his head. "I can't believe it, we were going to spend the first century exploring the Morglands, have a hell of a blast," he replied, still looking into the ground.

Nari felt bad, too. Boron, it was obvious he had a thing for her, but he never had a chance to actually say it. Then she had an idea. "Xy," she said, but no one had any idea of what she was talking about. "What about her?" Amanda asked her. "I heard that the gods came back in the blade apocalypse. If it's true, if they actually came back. Maybe we can pray and ask her for a favor. Maybe she can bring Boron back," she suggested. It was more than a long shot, but right now any kind of hope was better than the bleak feeling that surrounded them right now.

It was the faintest glimmer of hope, it was all he needed. "Yes. Maybe the Goddess can help," Talcen said and something in his broken brain was connecting the dots and he stood up. Ticcen looked at Nari in disbelief. She wanted to say a whole lot right now, it wasn't the right time. The look in Amanda's eyes was exactly the same. The only one who wanted to believe this idea was Talcen.

Nari was spouting anything that came to her mind, and that was the first thing she thought of. If anyone could help, Xy would be the one to do it. But the reports coming from the North were sketchy at best. People reported everything from silver, flying knights, smoke zombies and all manner of things. There was almost no chance that any of it was real. Now it had no choice but to be real for both of their sakes.

"Glad to see you're standing again. Izor has a place we can go, it's not far from here but it's a great place to make a last stand in you're interested in doing that," Thodon said to them and they all nodded in silent agreement. It took one of their own, this thing had to pay.

Their only regret was that it couldn't feel pain, or fear. Talcen especially wanted to make the Golem suffer for what it did, but that was impossible. Destruction would have to do.

"Lead the way," Talcen said and had renewed confidence and a sense of hope, no matter how small it was going to be, there was no way he was going to let go of his friend so easily. There was no way he was going to accept it was over yet. Not when there was a Goddess out there that could fix everything.

"We're going to a place called Dawn's wall," Thodon said and started walking. It's not close so be ready for anything," he said to them and walked into the dark. The hunter didn't feel safe with four, likely hungry vampires behind him. He felt safer with the golem, to be honest with himself. But right now, he had a job to do so he would do it.

"How do you know?" Amanda asked him as they walked. "Izor is telling me where to go, he says it's our best place to try and kill the golem," Thodon replied and didn't look back. He didn't know where this wall was. For all he

*Jesse Wilson*

knew it didn't exist until they loaded it up with whatever strange magic they had going on here.

Nari didn't see any communication device but the radio and he didn't see him use it at all. But there was that short amount of time they were distracted. She didn't hear anything either. She didn't like trusting Dwarves, but right now she didn't have a choice. "Well, if we're going, let's get to it. We're burning moonlight," Nari said and started to walk.

"Good, we'll avenge Boron, then get him back," Talcen said with an almost delirious smile.

83

# Chapter Nineteen

"I can't wait to meet Xy," Talcen said as they walked ahead, closer to Thodon. He was already feeling better about all of this. There was no reason in his mind that the Goddess would say no at this point. Ticcen and Amanda both looked and Nari as they walked.

"Ladies, you have something you want to say right now?" she asked them, it was hard not to notice them. "Lying like that is only going to make things worse, there's never been any evidence that Xy even exists," Amanda said and Ticcen didn't believe that, but she also didn't believe that a Goddess like that would have bothered with them, no matter what the situation was.

"Listen, if Xy doesn't show up at the end of all of this. Then that's on her. I didn't lie, not really. I just said what I had to. If you had a better suggestion I would have liked to hear it otherwise, bug off," she said and shook her head.

"Fine. I guess you have a point," Amanda had to agree. But it was a terrible way to do things. Ticcen didn't think it was a very good thing to do either, but it was better than being broken down. At least for now. There was no reason to argue it. And neither of them actually knew for sure, maybe Xy would show up, it was impossible to know for sure. It felt like anything was possible right now.

They walked without incident for another five minutes when fire burst out in front of them, blocking their path. "What in the hell is it now?" Thodon said, he was sick of this place and all of its tricks.

"I am Saziz, the fire elemental. I am going to kill you all," the fire said and erupted into a spiral of deep orange flames. "Well, okay, fire monster. Any suggestions?" Amanda asked and backed off. Thodon shrugged and decided to try something.

"Saziz, I know you're supposed to take us down and all. But I'm not a vampire. I know you can sense that. There is a golem on the loose and there is an emergency. Please let us pass," Thodon said. He acted as if he had talked to lots of elementals before and showed no fear but a healthy amount of respect.

Saziz's flames died out and there was a shape of a man standing before them dressed in an orange suit and his eyes were burning green. "You really are in trouble, this isn't how the script is supposed to go. Is a golem really following you?" he asked him and Thodon nodded. "Yes, it killed one of their friends. We could use your help," he said and the elemental crossed his arms and looked at the vampires. "I've done this gig for two hundred years because I was promised unlimited chances to wipe these parasites off the face of the world, and you want me to help them, Dwarf?" Saziz asked.

Thodon knew elementals didn't like anyone very much by nature. "Well. I was hoping you would help," Thodon replied and it was clear he dropped his gruff nature completely. It was replaced with a healthy dose of something that resembled fear.

Saziz turned his green eyes on the vampires behind him. "No, I will not help you. However, I won't kill you either. It's not as fun to kill vampires when they're all scared like this," he said and with that he dissolved into millions of sparks, ascending into the sky.

Thodon let out a sigh of relief. He was well aware they all could have died there. He didn't know what restrictions the thing had to follow, if any at all. "Come on, let's go," Thodon said and his gruff nature returned immediately.

"How many times have you done that?" Talcen asked and Thodon looked at him. "Too many times, Elementals are hardcore but reasonable, sometimes," he said and looked ahead, then he started walking again. If they waited too long he might come back and had changed his mind.

"That was a fire elemental, how in the hell were we supposed to beat that?" Amanda asked. She knew full well just what it could do. "I assume we would have had a lot more items at this point to be more prepared. Trials and what not. As we are right now we wouldn't have had a chance," Ticcen replied and that made sense to her. With the latest danger past them they were able to move forward. Thodon was sure not all of their threats would be so intelligent to deal with in the future.

Everyone was hoping that the destination was close by and there weren't any more surprises. On the other hand, if the golem was on their trail, it was sure taking its sweet time in getting to them. The urge to hurry or the feeling of danger was quickly fading away with each step they took. There was no particular reason it would come after them anyway.

It had plenty of other groups of vampires to hunt down. Talcen couldn't help but fell a little sorry for them. If they were all stuck on one place, they would be meeting their final death. Just like Boron, and just like him and never see it coming. Unlike them, Talcen had a plan that was, in his mind, impossible to fail.

# Chapter Twenty

"How long do we have to walk before we get there?" Talcen asked, he was getting impatient, frustrated and his anger over his friend was coming to the surface with every step. "I don't know. Stop asking already, will you?" Thodon replied and was getting just as annoyed. He didn't care that much about Boron but now he was ready to kill Talcen too. He was considering how to do it when suddenly a noise caught his attention.

"Stop," he whispered and the others did that. The tension suddenly returning in a hurry. "Trees, now," Thodon said and ran to the left side diving into the safety of the trees. The others did the same.

"Why are we hiding?" Amanda whispered. None of them knew what was going on. "Shh," Thodon said again and lowered himself closer to the ground. His eyes never losing sight of the darkness in front of them.

"I don't see anything," Nari said as quietly as she could. "Shh, no more talking," Thodon said desperately, the others couldn't see anything. None of this made sense to them and all of them were sure that their senses far exceeded his. If they didn't see or hear anything, how could he? None of this was making any sense.

"Look there, just beyond those trees up ahead," Thodon said, pointed. They all looked in that direction with their red eyes and didn't see anything but trees. "What?" Ticcen asked quietly. Then it made sense to him.

"It's a War horn," Thodon said and continued. "Its mechanical nature must hide it from your senses. It's the perfect trap. I don't know how they got it here but, damn, this thing is dangerous," Thodon said and tried to figure out how the best way to avoid it would be.

"They got a unicorn in here. How in the hell did they get one of them and keep it here?" Nari asked. First a fire elemental and now one of these. There was no talking to this thing. Unicorns were horrible things and now one was in their path. "No matter. I'll just grow and take care of it. This won't take long," Nari said and started to make her way from the trees.

"Wait, no, you've never seen one of these things before. It won't be that easy," Thodon tried to say but it was far too late. She had come out of the trees and started walking down the path. She still couldn't see the unicorn in the trees.

"Come on out, beast. I have a surprise for you," she said as she walked down the path. It didn't take long before steel unicorn stepped out into the path before her. It was taller than she was right now. "Oh," she said to herself and realized that this might not have been that great of an idea. She wasted no time and grabbed the pendant around her neck and started to pull it off.

The eyes of the War horn exploded with bright blue light and struck her in the chest.

The force of the impact knocked her off her feet and set her on fire. Nari screamed as she tried to put the fire out with her hands. "God damn it," Thodon said and rushed out of the trees. "Why is this happening?" he asked himself, not believing he was about to fight a unicorn, defending a vampire who was stupid enough not to listen to him.

He pulled his cannons off his belt and aimed as he ran forward. Thodon pulled the triggers and hit the unicorn in the face causing it to back off just a little. It wasn't enough to cause it harm or distract it. The cyborg nightmare, if it wasn't angry before, it was now. Thodon watched as it's back opened up and to his horror realized what was about to happen.

"Everyone, get the hell out of here, run," Thodon screamed and hoped that they were paying attention. The War horn stomped on the ground and fired off hundreds of projectiles, micro missiles that looked like shooting stars.

The others watched the display and realized that the target was literally everything in the area. "Oh, come on," Talcen said and realized the same thing they all did. The safest place to be was as close to the beast as they could get. "Run to the unicorn," Talcen screamed and they started to run in that direction. "This is the worst idea ever. If Nari lives through this I'm going kill her," Amanda said to herself. She was laying on the ground, still struggling with the fire. Amanda decided that she didn't mean it but still, this was all her fault and nothing was going to change that.

Ticcen ran out the trees but instead of making a straight path to the unicorn, she made a path to Thodon and Nari. Without thinking she took her shirt off and beat the flames out in a hurry. "Nice thinking," Thodon said, it was something that he couldn't do with the armor he had on. "Thanks," Ticcen said and put her shirt back on in a hurry.

Nari wasn't burned enough to be destroyed. Her chest and stomach was blackened and half of her face was burned too, her skin was black and flaking off. Ticcen put her arms under the burned woman, picked her up with ease despite her size. "Come on, we need to get out here," Thodon said and looked up. Those missiles were already on their way back down.

"There isn't anywhere to go but towards the monster," she said as they moved towards it. "Good," Thodon said and drew his sword. "I have to take care of this now," he said and intended to send the monster back where it came from. The missiles began to fall, the tops of trees and everything around them began to explode as they made impact.

The noise made communication impossible as the explosions took over everything around them. Thodon lost track of everyone as he focused on the living weapon in front of them. This missile barrage was just to get them all out of hiding. It was textbook War horn tactics.

Once everyone was close it would attack and attempt to kill everyone. It was just what they did, there was no way around it. Thodon knew that the obvious thing to do to avoid the missiles was run closer to the launch point.

It was also obvious none of these people had ever encountered anything like this before. They were falling right into its trap. Speed was the only thing he could do now and he ran as fast as he could to make his attack mean something.

"Go back to hell," Thodon screamed as he jumped forward, sword in hand. He swung toward the base of that horn and nothing was in his way. He was going to do this on one clean swipe. The blade got within inches of the horn and something stopped it. A forcefield that he didn't expect. "What in the hell is up with this?" he asked and couldn't believe that this was actually happening. The impact of the shield stopped him cold. He drew back as fast as he could and realized that everything here had to be enchanted somehow.

Only the vampires had a chance of winning here. Thodon was useless and worse now he was mere feet in front of a nightmarish unicorn that was going to rip his head off in one bite. There was no reason to believe that anything could save him now. "Well, I guess if you're going to die, this is the best way to do it," he said and almost smiled, but couldn't bring himself to do it.

It was then there was a blast that came from the left and knocked the metal horse to the side, displacing it enough to get Thodon away from that horrible mouth. "Keep running," Amanda yelled at him from a distance. It was clear she thought he was insane for even trying to attack the thing. Thodon took advantage of the distraction and quickly ran around the thing.

He could see from here that everyone else had the right idea, but they weren't going to wait around and stand next to the thing. They all intended to just keep running.

Thodon was used to fighting almost everything and he brought his experience from outside the walls to the inside. It was different here.

The dwarf ran as fast as he could and he didn't bother to look back in the sea of fire the monster had created. However, he could hear its metal hooves slamming against the ground. It had clearly decided to come after them and there was no reason to believe any of them could out run it. "Damn," he said to himself and knew that one of them needed to fight.

"Amanda, I need you to help me kill it. We can't out run it," Thodon yelled as he heard the distinctive spinning sound of two miniguns behind him. "Everyone, out of the way now," Thodon yelled and dove to the ground, rolled right off the path just as the weapon opened fire.

Thodon was in terrible danger, however the others were not. "Damn vampires," Thodon said as he watched the bullets fly through their dead flesh harmlessly as they stopped in their tracks. They lifted their arms as if the wind had picked up a little bit. "Oh, so you were shooting at me, I get it," he said to himself not sure if he should have felt special about any of that or not. All he could do now was keep his head down and wait for the gunfire to stop.

It didn't take long for it to stop and soon enough it looked as if Amanda and Talcen were ready to fight back. Ticcen still held the burnt Nari in her arms and stood farther down the path. "No, wait, you need to keep running. Don't worry about me, I'll catch up," Thodon yelled out to them but they weren't interested in running anymore.

"Damn," he said again, frustrated. Their inexperience was going to get them all killed, also he was pretty sure that a shotgun wasn't going to take a war machine like that down.

Thodon stood up and threw his blade in the direction of Talcen. "Catch," he yelled out and the vampire reached out and caught it by the handle with ease. "If you're going to kill it, you need to cut its horn off, no exceptions," Thodon yelled to them and started to make his way back toward Ticcen. He knew the two of them could handle the beast if they were careful, after all they would have to do it anyway to get to the battlegrounds.

This was their destiny or something like that. Or, all the same, they could have died here just the same. That was always a chance.

Talcen held the blade in both hands and Amanda aimed her weapon. The metal unicorn gazed into their red eyes with its own burning eyes. With no warning it opened its mouth and let loose a large cone of white flames. "Move," Amanda yelled and jumped to the side. Talcen dove in the opposite direction. The fire missed them both but it was hot enough to set the path itself on fire and everything else that it touched.

"How in the hell are we supposed to beat something like that?" Amanda asked as she watched the white fire burn everything it touched. She could feel the heat from here as if she were standing right next to it.

Talcen had never seen white flames like this before and was mesmerized for a second as he took it all in. He thought it was pretty cool, actually, impressive that something could create fire like this at all. He knew for a fact that Boron would have thought the same thing, too.

He shook his head and came back to reality. "Right, wake up man," he said to himself and gripped the sword tight. He knew what he had to do but timing was everything. It didn't seem to see him right now, if it had he was sure those twisting flames would be heading in his direction in a hurry. Talcen watched as the flames died out and the Unicorn looked around, scanning for its prey.

He saw Amanda in the dark and it was clear neither of them had any idea of what to do next. There was no plan here and that might have been what did them both in, in the end of all of this.

Then out of nowhere Amanda gave him a smile, a thumb up and started to walk back out of the trees. The war horn saw her, turned its head in her direction. "Hey, metalhead, I'm over here," she said to it and pulled the trigger.

The shot hit the unicorn in the side of the head and knocked it to the side. There was no real damage done to it, however, it was annoyed and let out a sharp screech of anger that sounded like dry metal rubbing against one another.

It was hard to listen to and now they were all thankful it didn't like to use its voice very often.

Talcen saw Amanda was using herself as bait here. A distraction and he wasn't going to let it go to waste. He crept out the shadows and prepared himself for battle. Amanda fired again and hit the horse in the neck. It screeched again and seemed prepared to dismember the annoyance with its metal hooves and teeth as it started to walk towards her.

"Oh, you stupid unicorn, you can't kill me. You were brought here for us to kill you. You're nothing more than a test," Amanda said and wondered how accurate this thing really was.

Was it a real unicorn or just a machine made to mimic one? She had heard stories of the monsters before and they were completely not this, they were far more aggressive, violent and horrible. This seemed like a mindless beast made to get in the way.

Either that or all the stories she heard were nothing more than just stories and that was it. People making stuff up for no reason.

Talcen started running and leaped forward. He put his sword as the base of the steel horn on the head of the thing. The blade carved through it and the unicorn screamed in surprise and pain. It started to buck wildly out of control. Talcen stood beside Amanda as they both took a few steps back, not knowing what to expect out of this.

The war horn shot one final blast of white flame at the two of them and Amanda pushed Talcen out of the way and tried to get out of the way. Most of her made it but her arm was caught in the fire. She screamed in pain, stumbled backwards as best as she could. The unicorn suddenly stopped moving, then it started to fall apart.

It was clearly obvious that this wasn't a real unicorn because all the parts were mechanical. There was no blood here at all as it fell to pieces. The whole process didn't take very long and soon it was just a pile of scrap metal on the path.

Talcen ran to Amanda who was doing her best to stand up. Her right arm was completely gone and she was in shock. "Hey, are you alright?" Talcen said and drew back a little when he saw just how bad her injury was. "Yeah, I'm going to be fine, just fine. Everything is okay," she said and began to fall over. Talcen caught her before she did. "I got you, don't worry," he said and didn't know why he said not to worry. They both knew that the danger was still coming in their direction. "Not worried, I'm just fine," Amanda replied and passed out, the shotgun fell to the ground and he caught her. "Come on," he said to himself.

"Thodon, I need you," Talcen cried out and hoped he was close enough to hear him. "Thanks," he said to Amanda who had given up her arm to save him from being killed. Even though they said death wasn't an issue, he was hard pressed to imagine how he would have lived through a direct blast of that fire. It really didn't make any sense to him but it didn't matter now.

"I'm here, kid, you did good," Thodon said as he came up to him and took his sword back. "Damn, she got fried," he said as he put the sword away. "Thanks for being so obvious," Talcen replied and continued. "Listen. She needs a few drops of blood to heal. I'm going to guess they both do and I only have one stone left in my pack. I don't know if one of them would help. You're the only thing with blood so it would be appreciated if you could help out right now," Talcen said and Thodon crossed his arms.

"Giving blood to a vampire is a dangerous thing. Sometimes they lose their minds if it's the first time and I for one would rather not be here when it happens, you understand?" Thodon replied. He knew full well what the risks were and basically, he would have to deal with all of it. The others were safe. "Come on man, one or two drops is all they need. It's not like I'm asking you to open your neck or anything," Talcen begged him again and the hunter sighed. "Fine," he said.

Thodon took his armored glove off and wasn't too sure how he should do this. He didn't have much that sharp besides the axe and the sword. He didn't see any non melted rocks that were useful. He didn't have to decide. Talcen had already set Amanda down. "Thanks," he said and grabbed Thodon's hand. With one swipe of a sharp fingernail he cut the Dwarf's flesh. "Ouch," Thodon said, this was unexpected but at least it was quick.

He watched as the bright red blood dripped into Amanda's mouth. "That's enough," Thodon said and pulled his hand back. He knew she would be healing soon and while he was still bleeding he figured that he would go help the one who caused all of this to begin with. "Thanks," Talcen said as he got up and walked away. Thodon didn't feel like he was doing a good thing over all. This was getting to be much more involved than he had ever intended.

Nari was on the ground, most of her was burned and she was still out cold. "Stand back," Thodon said and Ticcen did. The smell of fresh blood was easy to detect. There was nothing else like it and she was tempted to ask if she could have some too, but refused to do this. He held his bleeding hand over mouth and let some drops fall inside. The effect was immediate and Nari's eyes opened. She reached up, grabbed his wrist.

"Son of a Unicorn," he said in surprise and tried to fight her but Nari's power was overwhelming.

Ticcen quickly reached down and pulled Nari's hand off of his wrist. Thodon rubbed it and tested it to make sure nothing was broken. Thankfully nothing was, it just hurt. He put his armored glove back on in a hurry. Thodon watched as Nari sat up and she was healing quickly, but it was clear that she had never had real blood before.

Her eyes were all he needed to see that the blood madness had taken her completely. The vampire race was exceedingly violent at times. They had a dark beast inside all of them and sometimes the first time they got blood, the beast took over.

"Nari, I need you to listen to me. I'm not food. We are in serious trouble right now. I need you to wake up," Thodon said to her but acted as if he was talking to a wild animal, calmly, soft and slow as he could. It was clear that this wasn't going to work at all.

Nari lunged at him and He flinched. She cleared the distance between them in a second. Her hands were an inch away from his neck. Ticcen was right behind her. Holding her back. "Damn's she's strong," Ticcen said and was still being dragged forward bit by bit.

Nari's mouth was full of countless razor-sharp fangs and her eyes were wide and bright red. All of her former features were missing, replaced by dead white skin and fury. The beast inside of her had come out. Thodon backed off, he wasn't afraid anymore but still this was always dangerous. "If you have a fix to this now is the time," Ticcen said as she grit her teeth, straining to keep her held back.

Thodon clenched his right fist and punched Nari in the face as hard as he could. Nari's fangs shattered in her mouth and fell to the ground.

"Not my first time messing with an insane vampire," he said as Nari screamed in pain and immediately turned away. Her beast was gone and she was sobbing in pain and all kinds of other things, he supposed. Not too many people knew that even if they were undead, their fangs were still overly sensitive to pain when fully exposed.

"Sorry," Thodon said. He didn't want to do that but he didn't have any other choice in the matter. He looked to Amanda and she was already regenerating but not awake yet. "Talcen, pick her up, toss me the weapon. We are moving," he said to her and Talcen picked up the shotgun and threw it to him.

Thodon caught it with his cut hand and there was a dull amount of pain that traveled through his arm. He didn't show any sign of it. He looked at the weapon and realized that if this thing was capable of getting to the outside world, he was taking it with him. An infinite ammo shotgun would be priceless in his line of work. He wasn't about to let them know that.

"Let's keep moving and for the sake of the Gods, if we see anything horrible we can avoid, don't walk into it. That'd be really helpful for us staying alive," he said to them and no one responded. Hopefully that was obvious by now, Thodon wasn't going to count on it, however.

"What in the hell happened?" Amanda asked in a weak voice, her arm was sill regenerating and she couldn't really move. "You saved me from a fake unicorn, thanks," Talcen replied to her and nodded. "Are you carrying me, or is this some kind of weird afterlife. I feel like I'm floating," she said and smiled. "I am, you're lighter than you look," Talcen said and wondered if there really was an afterlife for vampires at all. If there was, he never heard of such a thing.

Amanda ignored the comment and turned her head towards the trees that were passing by in slow motion. She felt like she was getting a little better all the time as they walked down the path.

Nari's sense returned to her as her fangs were shattered. "What did I do?" she asked between sobs. "Nari, it's okay. You just went insane for a few seconds but you're fine now," Ticcen replied to her. "Insane, what do you mean insane?" she asked concerned and stopped crying. "Oh yeah. You were burned pretty bad so Thodon gave you a few drops of blood and the beast totally came out. You were awesome. Terrifying. I've never seen anyone go into beast mode so hard as you did," Ticcen said and she wasn't sure if she was supposed to be impressed or just scared.

Nari wasn't sure if she ever wanted blood again after that. Losing control like that was a stereotypical vampire trait that made all of them look bad. "Okay, well. Hopefully it doesn't happen again," she said and wiped the last of the burned skin away from her arm. "I need new clothes," she said and looked down. Everything she was wearing was torched, close to falling part.

"Did you bring some in your bag?" Ticcen asked her and Nari looked around. "I actually did, but where did I put it?" she asked and wasn't sure about that. She didn't see it anywhere. "Exran," Nari said and there was a white flash of light.

"Retraction spell. Nice," Ticcen said and noticed that the others were already on their way. It was clear that waiting up for them just wasn't an option right now.

"Make it snappy," Ticcen said and looked back to her. "I'll wait right here. No need for them to see you get changed anyway," she finished as Nari opened her bag and pulled clothes out of it. "Right. I'll make it quick," she said and started to tear her burned clothes off. They simply fell apart at the slightest force. Ticcen crossed her arms and looked between her and the rest of the group making sure no one was looking.

She was impressed with Nari, she was almost pure muscle under the ashen clothes. The giant race was physically impressive, but a vampire in the mix, she began to realize that maybe it wasn't hate that caused people to not like her, but just being intimidated in general was enough to do it.

Ticcen was able to remain stoic through the whole process. "Sorry about that," Nari said and sounded embarrassed at the same time.

"About what?" Ticcen asked, confused. "My body, it's pathetic I know. I used to be called scrawny and such by my people back before I was turned. Painful to look at," she said and Ticcen shrugged. "Well, one, you're not with them anymore so who cares what they think, two, you've got it where it counts. Don't be sorry about that ever again," Ticcen replied and Nari was shocked. "No vampire had ever said that to me before. Usually it is always 'no, cover up,' you know. But thanks," she replied and smiled. Ticcen found that really hard to believe but didn't want to argue the point right now.

"Come on, let's catch up with the others before that unicorn thing resets itself," Ticcen said and moved forward down the path. Nari zipped up her bag and followed her. Neither one of them wanted to be here when or that thing came back to life.

# Chapter Twenty One

Dawn's wall was nowhere in sight and Thodon was getting annoyed. That thing should have been close by but that was an hour ago. "Izor, where the hell is this place, our time is running out," he asked into his radio, but there was no reply. Thodon narrowed his eyes and began to believe that maybe all of them were being left out here to die after all.

Maybe they came up with a different plan to take care of the black bone golem, but needed it to tie up any loose ends. Silence was making him nervous. It always had.

"What's the matter with your radio?" Talcen asked. "Nothing, the people who called me here aren't answering. I think we've been played," he replied exactly what he was thinking. "We could be in a dead zone, too," Talcen replied, he didn't want to believe they would have been left to die like this. "We could be, I don't know this place well enough to know if there are any. I would think the people running it would need to be in constant communication. Dead zones in here shouldn't be a thing," he replied.

Thodon knew this place was nothing more than a deadly amusement park. It needed people to keep the scripted events running. "Well, everyone is going to start getting angry if we don't find a place to hide out soon. The golem is sure to be on our case soon. It's the only real monster in the place," Talcen said and Thodon knew all of this.

"Trust me. I know. I've been doing this for a long time and I really know, you don't need to tell me. All we can do is keep trying to contact them and hope we find this place before the thing does. That's literally all we can do. You are the most nervous vampire I've ever met, relax as long as we keep moving we'll be okay," Thodon replied to him. Talcen realized he was talking entirely too much for the situation.

He knew what desperate sounded like and Talcen was it. The others weren't saying anything right now but he could practically feel the desperation coming off of them as they walked.

He had no idea how many times he had been in this exact situation in the outside. Some idiot rookie adventurer looking for things ran into a golem and needed an escort back home. Most of those events had worked out too so this one was going to be just fine, too. At least this is what he was hoping for.

"With any luck you're right and we're just in a dead zone. I'm sure they'll get back to us soon," Thodon said and was doing his best to contain the panic that was growing inside of himself and Talcen. "Why don't you hang back and see how the others are doing?" Thodon said, really, he just wanted to be left alone but he needed a reason that didn't sound mean.

"Yeah, I can do that," Talcen replied and slowed down.

Amanda had regenerated and was fine, the other two had caught up as well. "Thodon says we're in a dead zone, but we should be to the wall at any time," Talcen said to the others. "I don't know about you but I could eat something," Amanda said and the rest of them were feeling about the same way.

"Me too," Ticcen said and really hated being hungry for any reason. "Guys, don't worry. Once we get to the wall I am sure there will be supplies for us there, more than enough," he said and they really wanted to believe him.

Thodon was going to try again when suddenly his radio came to life all on its own. "Thodon, come in, it's Bill," the voice said. He grabbed his radio and replied. "Thought you forgot about us, what is going on out here?" Thodon asked and there was silence on the other end.

"It's bad, the golem is on a killing spree on lots of other levels. Most of the other groups have been staked. They were in their safehouses and the thing just, well, broke through the walls and wiped them out one at a time," Bill replied and Thodon couldn't believe it, now he knew why it didn't come after them. It was busy.

"We need the wall, Bill. Load it up for us and we'll be okay," Thodon said and more silence. "Izor is missing. After the safe houses began to fall the guy lost it and ran off somewhere. He hasn't been seen in an hour and its complete chaos up here. The military wants to know what is going on and I don't know what to tell them. I can get the wall up for you and supplies but there is no chance that it will stop the golem. I've also opened up the magic barrier for you, but just your level, it's all I can do. I'm sorry," Bill said and the radio clicked off.

"Bill, hey man don't," he stopped talking, it was pointless. Thodon was mad that the elf had to die, he was sure that he had some kind of magic that might have been higher level. Thodon had a couple of spells but he was pretty sure that they weren't anything that was going to be enough to stop this kind of golem for very long.

The five of them felt the earth rumble beneath their feet moments later and they stopped. "Is it the golem?" Nari asked and looked around in a hurry, afraid all of the sudden. "No, no it isn't. Look," Amanda said and pointed. The fog in front of them that no one had noticed before separated and there it was. A shining, but old looking wall. "Why is it glowing, why is it so hard to look at?" Ticcen asked and shielded her eyes.

"It's called Dawn's wall, it's made out of sunstone," Thodon said and kept walking forward towards it. "Don't ask me why it's here. I don't know, but it's our best defense against the thing that is coming for us, we need to get inside," he said to them and the others hoped that it wasn't this bright inside. "Sunstone, what the hell kind of place needs to be made out of that?" Talcen asked, but no one had any answers.

The closer they got to it, they all realized that it not a wall, but a fortress. There was a large door in front of them and it ended with guard towers on both ends. "Come on," Thodon said and walked to the door. It looked big and heavy, made out of the same stone as the rest of it, but he simply pushed it open. It slid open without trouble at all.

"I expected more resistance," Nari said and shrugged. To their relief the second it opened there was only darkness with in. It was a welcome sight.

"Everyone inside," Thodon said and stood beside the door. He needed to be sure everyone made it inside and no one was thinking of trying anything stupid. "What a gentleman, letting all of us go first," Amanda said and Thodon just nodded in response. Nari still couldn't look at him for what she did earlier, but he hardly cared.

He wasn't the kind to hold on to the little things like that and ignored it. Ticcen was the last one to get inside. With the last one in he quickly closed the door behind them.

Thodon's eyes adjusted to the dark and saw there was a gate lock for it. He pulled the chain and the large beam of silver slammed down into the brackets.

"There. Nice and secure," he said but it didn't make him feel any better. The golem could tear through that, but at least they would hear it coming.

"Okay, I don't know what this place is, exactly but I am going to need you all to explore, find any supplies you can and get armed. This golem..." he trailed off. Did he want to tell them what it was doing this whole time and why they haven't been attacked. Was it worth it to make them all hopeless now, no, not now.

"This golem is very powerful so you're going to need to find everything of use that you can. They unlocked the magic restriction too so if you know any spells, they could help, don't be afraid to use them," Thodon recovered and tried to go with the better option here.

The four of them looked around. There were only two directions to go but the place felt, like everything else so far, bigger on the inside. No one was questioning it anymore.

"I doubt there'll be any monsters in here so we can split up, but we better not take too long," Amanda said, she didn't want to be caught searching when the thing showed up, if it ever did. At this point she was starting to think they were safe and this whole journey was for nothing after all.

"Talcen and I will go left, you two go right. We'll meet back here as soon as we can so don't get lost," Ticcen said and there was no reason why she was in charge all of the sudden but no one really cared what direction they went in.

"I'll wait here," Thodon said was happy to finally get a break. He felt as if he had been walking for miles without stopping in a world of unending sameness. "Alright, we'll be right back," Amanda said and Nari nodded.

The two groups didn't waste any time and started to go down their separate directions, disappearing.

"Hurry back," Thodon said and walked a little way into the dark and found a bench there. He sat down and sighed, it was time to relax just a little bit. Of course, the truth was the same as it had always been. The second you relaxed was just about the same time that all hell tended to break loose around him, but he needed to anyway.

# Chapter Twenty Two

Amanda and Nari wandered off into the dark and they had no idea what to expect in this place. "Can you imagine how many thousands of others have been right here where we are. I wonder what kinds of stories they had to share," Nari said and looked around. She could only imagine the untold history this place had.

"I'd rather focus on our right now instead of thinking about the past that can't help us right now," she replied as they walked.

Nari just shrugged and figured it was her loss. History was a thing she liked and it was hard to be in a place that was so important and just not wonder about it. It was long that Amanda spotted a door, it was made out of wood and looked as if it was ancient. It blended in with the rest of this place rather well.

"Let's try that one," she said and pointed. Nari saw it and once again her imagination ran wild with what might be behind that door. It could have been anything at all. Amanda was hoping it was something to eat because she was starving. It was getting hard to hold back the urge to simply attack Thodon and drink him.

Amanda got to the door first and opened it. She expected it to squeak or groan. Offer even some resistance. The door swung open as if has been used a lot and someone was taking care of it. They didn't need any lights to see inside of this place. Actually, besides the entrance and the outside, there was no light in here at all, anywhere.

"Weapons," Amanda said with a smile. It wasn't food, but it was a good second best. An arsenal of things that were useful. But there were so many that the five of them couldn't possibly use them all. Nari got an idea.

"Let's take them all, I think I know of something that will work for us," she said and smiled. Amanda had no idea what she was thinking of and it forced her to ask. "What in the world are you thinking about?" she asked and Nari just nodded. "Don't you worry. Just help me get all of the weapons we can out of here. We should be strong enough to take them all with us between the two of us," she said and Amanda still was lost.

"Fine, I'll help you," she said and looked around. "However, I don't feel like carrying everything back to the entrance," she said and looked for anything that would help them out in their task. Nari saw her point, just because they were strong enough to do it didn't mean they could balance the piles or make it back without spilling. If time was of the essence, there was no room for stupid mistakes. Nari. "Hey, look over there. I think that's a net," she said and pointed.

"You're absolutely right," Amanda replied and walked into the room.

She moved to the net and pulled it off the hook it was hanging from. "This thing's huge," she said and had no idea just what it might be used to catch. They didn't see anything that big around here in their travels but then again this was far from normal. Amanda walked back out to the hallway and Nari helped her unfold the net and spread it out as best as they could.

"Alright, let's load up as much as we can get in here," Nari said, still smiling. Amanda still had no idea what her plan was but arguing right now was a waste of time.

The two of them walked back into the armory and took to opposite sides. At once they started to take the weapons off the walls and bringing them back to the net. They were doing their best to keep them all organized so when they pulled the net they just didn't fall out everywhere along the way back.

Ticcen and Talcen walked down their own similar and dark path. "I don't know about you but I'm pissed about all of this," Talcen said and she rolled her eyes at his words. She knew this already, well aware of his broken record feelings about all of this.

"Vampires are supposed to be emotionless," Ticcen replied and tried to bring up a good point. "You know as well as I do that the emotions never go away," he replied. "I know that, but right now I am getting pretty sick of yours. I get it. You are mad, so am I. I didn't like Boron as much as you did but still, he shouldn't have died like that," she replied and Talcen almost admitted to himself that maybe he was holding on to this a little too tightly.

"Xy will help me out, anyway," Talcen said and he smiled about that. The slim sliver of hope was keeping him encouraged. "When was the last time you read a book on what Vampires really believe. I know that neo's like us aren't allowed to be in the religion until we pass this last test but really. What do either of us know. I doubt Xy even exists at all. The gods are just made up fairy tales to keep all the races in line. That's it," Ticcen replied and Talcen stopped in his tracks.

"No, that's not right," he replied. "I have to believe that there is something stronger than us out there. Something that makes all of this mean something. If she doesn't exist then where did we come from, how did we get started?" he asked and she turned around and shrugged. "Who cares. Maybe we've always been on this planet. But don't be crushed when she doesn't show up to bring Boron back to life, okay?" she said to him and he looked to the floor.

"Fine," he said weakly. He still believed in the power of the goddess, he still believed that everything was going to be okay.

"Come on, I thought I saw a door ahead," she said, turned and kept walking forward. Talcen shook his head and banished his thoughts. "Yeah, okay," he replied and caught up to her in a hurry. Sure enough, she did see a door there in the distance and it didn't take them long to get to it. "I wonder if this is trapped," Ticcen said and looked around the edges to see anything obvious. This place has been nothing but a big deathtrap so far so this place shouldn't have been much different.

Talcen didn't want to waste time looking. He was sure this place wasn't trapped so he walked to the door, put his hand around the handle and pushed it in. The door swung forward with no resistance and no explosion, either. Ticcen recoiled at the action, but was relieved when nothing happened. Talcen walked inside without even thinking twice about it.

"Oh, you got to come in here," he said and was immediately excited about something. Ticcen wasn't sure what she was seeing but tried to contain her own excitement.

"Bloodstones, so many," he said and she saw it too. There were buckets filled with bloodstones. The two of them walked forward and they each grabbed one. At about the same time they sunk their fangs into the stones and drank the artificial blood that was inside. Immediately both of them felt normal and didn't realize how hungry they actually were.

"So good," Talcen said as he pulled the empty stone from his mouth and tossed the casing to the side. Ticcen finished too and smiled. "It'll do just fine," she said in agreement grabbed another one. She proceeded to sink her fangs into it as well. Talcen did the same thing, there were plenty to go around.

Within minutes the two of them were completely full. "I haven't eaten that much in ages," Talcen said and looked around the room. There appeared to be hundreds more. This place was built to house vampires for a long time. Just how long was Stone Tooth supposed to take, anyway? Talcen thought and had no idea how any of this was supposed to work.

"We need to bring a couple of baskets back for the others," Ticcen said and he nodded. "Yeah, we need to do that, I'm sure they are starving," he added and picked up a basket. Then he noticed a basket full of black stones. "Hey, what do you suppose these are?" he asked his sister who turned and looked at them.

"No idea. There is a whole basket full of them so I'll take one of the normal ones and you take one of them," she said and continued. "Maybe Thodon will know, he seems to know a lot of things," she suggested. It made sense. "Sounds like a plan to me," he replied and smiled. They picked up their baskets and walked back towards the door. Ticcen didn't bother to close it behind her. Past this door, the black hall stretched onwards as far as they could see. There was no telling what was over there and there was no time to go look.

"Come on, let's go back," she said and the two of them left the unknown behind.

# Chapter Twenty Three

Thodon waited alone, he liked the peace for a time. It gave him a chance to recharge and get something to eat. He waved his hand in the air, a thin blue line appeared below his hand. He reached inside and pulled out a sandwich.

"Finally," he said and started to eat. It was good and it was the first thing he'd really eaten all day. Those vampires might only need blood to live but he needed a little more and didn't want to go on to the menu. He hoped they had found something to eat because it wouldn't be much longer before he had no choice but to defend himself.

His sandwich didn't take very long to finish off, he reached into the line again and pulled out a bottle of water. It wasn't his favorite choice but this was no time to drink anything that was going to mess with his head. He twisted off the cap and drank half of it in one shot. It was cold and perfect, just how he imagined it to be.

He wasn't sure if he should be nervous about this or not. The longer it took the worse it was going to be when it finally came. There was no if about it. That golem was out there, walking in their direction. He could feel it.

He drank the rest his water when from one side he heard the sound of dragging metal. "It didn't get in, did it?" he asked himself and stood up. This didn't sound like a golem but there was no telling what lurked inside of this place waiting for them. He was ready for anything that might be coming his way. He tensed up and looked into the dark, wishing his vision was as good as his vampire traveling partners about now.

"We're back!" Amanda yelled out and Thodon relaxed a little bit, but he didn't know what they found, it sounded heavy and dangerous. He was going to ask when his question was answered for him right away. He could see in the dim light from nowhere that it was weapons. Lots of them.

"Okay, so what do you plan to do with all those guns?" Thodon asked and he was impressed, but confused. "No idea, ask the mastermind back there," Amanda said and had to step back. She couldn't help but notice how good Thodon was beginning to smell from here and she wanted to just tear into him right now. He noticed her eyes were beginning to look more like a predator by the second.

"My plan is that more is always better. If that golem is as strong as it looks, we're going to need all the help we can get. If it can't get in here we can attack it from on top of the wall. There must be away to get up there. I'd say we got this whole situation taken care of," Nari said and crossed her arms.

"Well, I didn't see any way to get up there but if you can find one that seems like a good plan to me," Thodon replied and was seriously wishing the other two would get back. Maybe they had something that was going to keep him alive a little longer.

"I didn't see a way up either but I'll find one. I am really good at finding things," Amanda said and looked around. There weren't any ladders or stairs close by. "I might have to look a little harder for this one," Amanda finished and Thodon didn't care, if this was the plan he could get them on top of the wall with his teleportation rune, but anything to keep them distracted a little longer, he was all for that plan right now.

Five seconds felt like five hours with Amanda staring at him like she was doing. But just when he was reaching for his sword, footsteps from the other direction.

"Hey, we found some bloodstones. It's lunch time," Ticcen yelled out of the dark. "I found some black ones, we don't know what the difference is but grabbed some anyway," Talcen said next and the others looked at one another.

"Food, I almost forgot how absolutely starved I really was," Nari said and those bestial eyes began to return ever so slightly. The two of them came into the dim light and set their baskets down. The vampires might have liked the sight of them, they just saved his life. Thodon quickly stepped out of the way as the other two approached the food.

Neither one bothered to grab a black stone as they quickly grabbed and bit into the red ones. Thodon felt much safer now that they all had something to eat that wasn't him. Vampires were the personification of the word hangry.

Thodon had no idea what the black ones were all about. He'd never heard of such a thing either and the limited experience he had with vampires, if they knew, they had never mentioned it either. "I would hold off on trying those black ones, we have no idea what they do and they might not be good for you," Thodon said.

"Sounds good to me," Nari said, she was eyeing them suspiciously. The others weren't too eager to try something new.

It was then Talcen noticed all the weapons on the ground. "Holy snorb, where did you get all the firepower?" he asked and they shrugged. "We cleaned out an armory down the hall. We got everything we could see inside the room. That golem is going to be bone dust by the time we're done with it," Nari said and Amanda finished her stone, tossed it to the side.

"If anything can live through all of this firepower, it deserves to kill us," she said and Thodon raised an eyebrow at that. "Dangerous words there, lady," he replied and she just shrugged. None of them wanted to die here, nor did they think that anything deserved to kill them.

"Oh, don't mind me. It's just the blood high," Amanda said and she hadn't eaten in quite a while and sometimes the sudden rush made her over confident. "Fair enough, but still, let's not die out there today, alright?" Thodon said looked up before continuing. "I can get all the weapons to the roof but, did anyone check to see if they were loaded at all?" he asked them. Nari and Amanda looked at one another. It was obvious that they hadn't checked.

"Um, well. I don't know," Amanda said and looked down at the guns. She bent over and picked up an assault rifle, she had no idea what kind it was but it looked like every one she had ever seen. She pressed the button and the clip fell out. There were bullets inside of it. "Looks loaded to me," she said but didn't want to check all the others.

"Well, I guess we can assume that they are loaded, of course you should always assume that. Basic safety practice and all," Thodon said and the others looked at him and couldn't believe he just said that.

"We're not kids. We know how guns work," Ticcen said. Talcen really didn't know how guns worked, he didn't like the things but just went with it for now. Actually, with all the weapons on the ground, he was feeling pretty nervous about them.

He wasn't sure what they would be used for. Vampires weren't hurt by normal bullets, but maybe these were Prolexan bullets. Holy things made to kill vampires. It was the only thing he could think of.

No one else seemed to have the same thoughts as he did and they all seemed pretty relaxed by all of there on the floor like this. "Alright. Operation Kill the Golem is now in effect. We'll head to the roof and get ready," Thodon said and continued. "Wrap the net up and give it to me. I can teleport us up there," he said and held out his hand.

Nari immediately did that and she handed the corners of the net to him. He grabbed hold of it with one hand and grabbed hands with Amanda. "Link up," he said to them and one by one they all grabbed hands. "Wait a second," Talcen said and he reached over to grab the basket full of red stones. "Okay now," he said as he picked it up. There was a white flash and all of them were then gone.

# Chapter Twenty Four

The five of them reappeared on top of the wall and just like before it was glowing bright. "Oh man I can't see a thing," Amanda said and shielded her eyes just like the rest of them did in a hurry. "Vampires, you never have a decent pair of sunglasses when you need one, where is your Noxite?" Thodon asked them and It was something they hadn't needed since they got here.

"Pocket," Nari said with her eyes clenched shut. She pulled out her pendant and put it around her neck with the other one. The others did the same.

Almost immediately the Noxite began to do its job and sparkle blue, cancelling out the glare of the sunstone. "Does anyone know why this is here in a vampire training camp?" Talcen finally asked, but none of them did.

"I assume it's to simulate siege battle conditions against something else that doesn't like the light. Teamwork under pressure and all that stuff," Amanda suggested the only thing that made sense to her.

"I just hope that we don't meet whatever force this place was planned to defend against any time soon," Talcen said.

Thodon dropped the net. "Everyone take a weapon and run down the wall, set it up against the wall so it's ready to use. We have no idea what we are going to face so mobility is extremely important," Thodon said to them and they started to do pick up guns. They looked the same. Thodon noticed one that was round and bigger.

"Hmm," he said as the others picked up the weapons.

Thodon picked the round gun up and it was heavy. "Well look at this," he said and smiled. It was a mini turret gun, and better yet the thing wasn't decaying anymore when he touched it. He unfolded the legs that were tucked up against it and set it up. Then on the side of it he saw that there was the same enchantment on the shotgun.

"Perfect," he said and looked at the others. "I will man this gun and set up shop here in the middle. You four set up along the wall and if we work together we shouldn't have a problem," he said and they nodded.

Talcen grabbed two weapons and started to follow his sister. There was no one else that he wanted to be close to in a situation like this this. Ticcen didn't really care where he went, just as long as he didn't end up shooting one of them on accident. This was entirely possible knowing him. Right now, it felt like the five of them were prepared for anything.

A few minutes into taking weapons to areas, something small and black could be seen coming their direction. "Hey, what's that?" Amanda asked, she noticed it first and the others looked in the direction she was pointing towards. "It's here," Thodon said and knew that it couldn't be anything else in the world. It was time to make their last stand here.

# Chapter Twenty Five

"Get ready," Thodon said the obvious as the black spot on the horizon kept walking in their direction. At this rate it would take forever to get to them but there. "It's the slowest thing I've ever seen," Nari said as she watched it. "Golems don't give a damn how long it takes to kill their targets. They are persistent. I hope you're a good shot," Thodon replied but he knew that this whole thing was unlikely to work.

His only hope was that they could do enough damage to the monster for him to take it down once and for all. The others seemed confident enough they could win.

"It's five on one, there is no way we can lose this fight," Amanda said, she was staring into the distance and trying to imagine how it might actually beat them. All the situations she thought resulted in a win for them, an easy win.

"Over confidence is a bad thing," Nari replied to her and picked out her weapon from the ones leaning on the wall. "No such thing as over confidence, Nari. We have this one in the bag, you'll see," Amanda replied to her and Nari just shrugged.

"I hate guns," Talcen said as he couldn't decide what weapon to use. "I can't believe you play all those silly war games on the Game station but when it comes to the real thing all you can do is complain," Ticcen replied to him and he shot a glance. "Hey, those games aren't real. All you have to do is push a button or two. Playing those things doesn't turn everyone into a gun nut you know," he replied and she sighed.

"Listen. This is how this works," she said and picked up a weapon. "You aim with this," she pointed at the sights. "You shoot with this," she pointed at the trigger. "Think of it like a game. All you have to do is press this button, that's all," she said and thrust the rifle into him.

"I know how it works, I guess," he said and took the weapon in his hands. It felt weird in his hands and he didn't like it either. "No choice, brother. We need to take this thing down. For Boron and to save ourselves, you know?" she asked him and Talcen narrowed his eyes.

"Yeah, for Boron," he said and tried his best to feel good about what came next.

"Oh, don't let the noise bother you too much. It's going to be loud. Just don't lose focus," she said to him. "I guess the old military life never really dies," Talcen said and she smiled. "Nope, it never really does. I was just lucky it was all boring patrols and stuff like that," she said and took aim. Looking through her scope she could see the Golem walking in a steady, but slow pace right in their direction. It's purple, burning eyes were strange to look at.

They only reminded her of Boron, however and his stupid choices that lead to this. She wished he was alive just so she could stake him for a few decades for this. Sure, he died, but Ticcen was sure that. Suppressing her rage, she made sure to concentrate on the now and be ready for anything.

Thodon looked to the left and right. The vampires looked as ready as they were ever going to be.

Thodon never took his eyes off of the golem in the distance when suddenly it disappeared. "What in the hell?" he asked himself and thought the place was finally getting to him. He glanced to the left and right. The reaction of the others clearly meant he wasn't seeing things. Would it appear on top of the wall? Thodon was extremely worried that they had just put themselves into a death trap.

"There it is," Amanda yelled and pointed down on the ground. It had stepped through space, teleported to their location and stood below them. But now it wasn't moving.

"Do we shoot at it?" Talcen asked quietly. "I don't know. Maybe it can't see us up here," she replied. The wall was very bright and maybe it hid them from whatever it used to scan for them. "Yeah, maybe," Talcen replied, he wasn't sure that made any sense but there was no other reason for it to stop that he could see.

"So, what do we do?" Nari asked, she was confused at the whole thing too. "I don't know but I don't think we should shoot at it. Maybe the sunstone is screwing with its eyes or whatever," Amanda replied and Nari didn't believe that for a second.

Thodon was nervous. There was no way that sunstone could have blinded it, could it be the case though? He had no idea, not really. No one was shooting and he was sure that they were thinking the same thing he was right now. It was a waiting game for right now, who would flinch first. Thodon had never faced a golem like this before and he simply had no idea what to do next.

The golem stood there below the burning wall and saw the shield around it. The teleportation tactic wouldn't work here. Its deadly brain was thinking of a new solution, and it was only a few seconds of time later until he found one that was sure to work. It took one step back and outstretched its arms. The ground exploded with dark green fire.

Thodon watched the green flames come out of the ground and began to get very nervous about the whole thing. It got even worse as he watched over three hundred figures rise out of the fire. "What in the world?" he asked himself as they did this.

"I've seen some of these people before," Amanda yelled out and continued. "They came from the busses. They're all vampires," Amanda said and on closer inspection the others could tell she was right.

Talcen looked and to his horror, there in the crowd he saw Boron rising from the fire again, but he was nothing like he was. He had no eyes and his mouth hung open slightly.

"That monster turned them all into mindless shades," Talcen said and hated it even more now. There were other shades there too. Vampires of all races in clothes several hundred years out of date, old military uniforms mostly. "There are so many," Ticcen replied and prepared to shoot.

Amanda saw this and began to panic. Shades were just mind controlled constructs, zombies, and she was terrified of stuff like this. She never could explain why. They were faced with an army of her personal nightmare now and there was nowhere to run to. "I think it sees us," Nari said and Amanda refused to reply to that obvious statement.

The fire went out and was replaced by a white mist that hung around their feet. The silence didn't last long as the first wave of shades started running towards the wall with a dreadful moan. "Fire, don't wait for me," Thodon yelled at them and pulled the trigger. His weapon came to life with rapid fire and he watched as a cluster of the shades fell into the mist as they were shredded.

He almost smiled, this was going to be too easy. He almost said it out loud when the group he brought down started to stand back up. "God damned vampires," he muttered to himself and took aim once again.

Talcen wanted to freeze. He was sure his sister was going to take care of everything, part of him was anyway. The other part knew better and forced him to pull the trigger. The gun wasn't as bad as he thought it would be. He watched as his bullet sailed harmlessly into the mist, disappearing. "Right," he said and took aim.

They were running right at him making it easy to aim. He pulled the trigger again and watched a hole get blasted through one of them. It staggered back, but then that wound closed up and he clenched his teeth. "So much for being special bullets," he said to himself and fired again.

Ticcen wasted no time in opening fire. The shades were fast but not agile. She aimed for the head of one of the things, fired. The decayed, broken head exploded and the shade fell into the mist. She waited for it to get back up, but it didn't seem to be getting up very fast.

"Headshots seem to keep them down longer, bro. Aim for the head if you can," she said to Talcen and fired again, but missed. "Damn," she said and vowed to do better next time.

Nari had no trouble shooting into the crowd, but she wasn't aiming all that well. "Woman, please. Aim better. Don't waste that many shots," Amanda managed to say as she watched the horde keep getting closer. "Shut up and shoot something, will you?" Nari replied but didn't bother to stop doing it.

Amanda took aim and was about to fire when one of the shades got close enough to jump. It leaped through the air and it was going to land on the wall. "Shoot it, now," Nari yelled and Amanda stared into the empty eye sockets as everything felt like it was moving in slow motion. She pulled up her gun and pulled the trigger.

Too late, the bullet hit the chest of the monster and went right through it. "Damn it," Amanda said as she got out of the way and watched the dead thing slowly start to move and try to stand up again. "No," she said and rushed back, away from the thing.

Nari slammed her foot into the back of its head and straight into the sunstone. She did this without thinking about it and the body of the shade collapsed. The body dissolved into the same white mist, blowing away in a breeze that didn't exist.

Once she saw these weren't what they appeared to be, her confidence returned just to where it had been before. Amanda rushed to the wall and started to fire weapon when two more leapt over the wall Nari turned her weapon and shot both of them in the face. The bodies flew forward and smashed into the wall behind the two of them and dissolved a few seconds later.

"Thank me when it's over," Nari said and quickly shot another one in the head that was about to jump in their direction. Amanda would remember to do that and she got back to the line and was determined to do her best to not let it break again.

Thodon knew that this plan was never going to work. He held the trigger down and was holding the center of the line back well enough. However, the turret was made to suppress an enemy and was very inaccurate. He was tearing their bodies to pieces but the bullets were missing the head completely. Also, this was just the first line.

There was a whole mess just waiting to come at them. This first line was nothing more than a test run of their defenses and it already wasn't going very well for them.

He watched then as the rest of the shades did exactly what he was afraid they would do. They all started to charge in their direction at one time.

"Well, it was fun while it lasted," he said to himself. On the other hand, he didn't want to give up either. Then Thodon got an idea that was crazy enough that it just might actually work.

# Chapter Twenty Six

"Everyone, listen to me. We can't stand here. Everyone follow me to the end of the wall. I have a plan," Thodon tried to yell over the gunfire, but it was pointless. He was frustrated with all the noise and he knew they didn't stand a chance. He stopped shooting and ran down the wall to Nari and Amanda. "Hey, listen. We are going to be over run. Follow me. I have a plan," he said and Amanda looked at him. There was no time to argue. "Fine, let's go," she replied as her and Nari grabbed another gun leaning against the wall. Amanda did the same thing.

The three of them started to move down the wall as fast as they could. Only a few seconds after they abandoned the post the mindless shades came up and over the wall. "Don't look back just get to the end of the wall," Thodon said as they ran past him.

He stopped at his turret gun and picked it up. This was essential to his plan. He picked the thing up when an arm came around his neck and pulled him back.

"No," he said to himself and pulled forward. The shades were much stronger than they looked and kept pulling him back. He struggled to free himself but another hand grabbed his left wrist. He wanted to yell out for help but at the same time didn't want to waste the time.

"Take the gun. Defend the end of the wall and bottleneck these bastards until there aren't any left," he yelled and when he did Nari turned around without breaking her stride in the slightest and ran at him as fast as she could.

Thodon was sure she was coming back for the weapon but she shot the shades holding on to him and the gunfire was so close that immediately his hearing was replaced by a loud, high pitched ring and nothing else. Nari grabbed his arm and pulled him forward. Everything was in slow motion right now but he did his best to hold on to the gun as best as he could. It was the one, most important thing right now.

Talcen and Ticcen noticed what was going on. Amanda pointed to the opposite end. Screamed something he couldn't hear. Thankfully no one was too eager to argue and soon they were all running in the same direction. Thodon couldn't hear anything, but he could feel the vibrations of the horde just behind them.

The end of the wall ended in a round tower, defendable from all sides. Thodon hoped they understood the plan now. He turned around and set up the gun again at in the main entrance. They were almost on them now. A steady stream of conjured demons had mindlessly followed them and kept jumping on the wall to join the others.

Thodon pulled the trigger, that gun came to life. He held the trigger and watched as the things in front of him exploded, fell back in the narrow path. To his horror they only started to reform and get back up. Amanda saw what he was doing, put her hand on his shoulder to get his attention. She pointed at her head and hoped that got the message across. Thodon understood, not only that he wondered why he didn't think of it himself.

He angled the weapon up just a few inches and watched the bullets start hitting their mark. The heads of the things began to explode, then the bodies followed as they dissolved into nothing. "Finally," he said to himself and wasn't sure how loud he was. He supposed no one was paying attention to him anyway, at least he hoped not.

The others were too busy to listen. The horde of things were climbing up the tower as fast as they could, and they were shooting them down. "These things are endless," Nari said as she shot another in the head. "Yeah but at least we can have an easier time of it," Amanda replied. 'Oh, you have a funny view of what the word easy actually means," Nari replied.

"Will you two shut up and focus?" Talcen asked them. He didn't care about the talking so much, he was just being distracted and now was not a very good time for anything like that. "Sorry," Amanda said and fired again.

"No, I'm sorry. It's just tense right now," Talcen replied and he didn't know how to feel about all of this but lashing out at them wasn't the right thing to do and he knew it.

Amanda smiled and understood where the sudden outburst came from. Ticcen screamed as a shade leapt forward. She fired and missed. The thing grabbed her by the neck and started to pull her off the edge. Talcen dropped his weapon and rushed to her side. The thing that was pulling her down was stronger than he was and he felt her slipping away. Ticcen was struggling to escape as more of the things started to climb up the wall.

"Talcen. Take my gun and shoot them as I fall. I'll be fine," she said in a hurry. Realizing this was going to get them all killed. "I can't," he said but she wasn't giving him a choice. Ticcen leapt of the wall and took all the things that were hanging on with her. Talcen picked up her weapon and started shooting the things as they fell into the mass of horror below. He didn't think much about it as he leapt off the wall after her.

"Son of a bitch," Nari said as she glanced to her right and saw the whole thing take place in a matter of seconds. She ran to Thodon and pulled the enchanted shotgun off his makeshift holster on his back, ran back to the place they fell and tossed the weapon down to them just as they hit the ground.

"Catch," she yelled as the swarm started to close in. She took aim with her gun and shot the two closest too them in the head to try to buy them a few more seconds.

The shotgun fell through the air. Talcen looked up and to him it only looked like a shiny black sliver of metal in a deep red night. He punched a thing in the face, knocking it back. He reached up and grabbed the weapon, pulled it down and gripped it in both hands. Then he began to fire as fast as he could, in all the directions. He never stopped to think what he was doing, right now he only had one thought on his mind. He had to save his sister and nothing else mattered.

# Chapter Twenty Seven

Talcen fired as many times as he could pull the trigger but still the horrible things pushed in towards him. Then he lost his mind. "Damn it, Xy. You lazy bastard where are you now?" he screamed at no one. He was furious at everything right now. Ticcen was already standing up, backing away towards the wall.

Then, everything froze in place. "Did you just call me a lazy bastard?" a voice asked him. Talcen's pale green skin felt like it was turning bone white with fear. "I think you did," she said again to him. Talcen turned and looked slowly. A woman was standing there in a black dress, black mist flowed under and around her constantly. "Xy, is that really you?" he asked and immediately regretted everything he just said. No one ever expects a Goddess to actually show up.

"Yeah. It looks like you have a little problem. I haven't seen a dread knight class golem up and running around, well, since the last one. Let me guess, it wasn't you right?" Xy asked him and Talcen was about to tell the story. She spoke up before he could answer. "I already know. Your idiot dead friend started all this," she said and crossed her arms.

"No one could have known what would happen, speaking of that idiot friend— "Talcen trailed off, he didn't know how to ask now that he had a chance to do it. "Yes?" she asked him, this time he was going to make him say it. "Could you bring Boron back to life, the monster killed him. I can't lose him he was my best friend," Talcen asked and said it the best way he could.

Xy sighed and shook her head. "You know. Generally, that's not my thing. He already got a chance to be eternal and wasted it," she said in a cold voice. "But I'll make you a deal. If you can take the golem down I'll bring him back," Xy replied to him. Talcen looked at the goddess in disbelief. "Thanks," it was all he could say right now, turned and faced the monsters who were still frozen in place and prepared to fight again.

"You know, you could have asked for another favor," Xy said with a laugh and wasn't sure if he was impressed or the little vampire just didn't think to ask after she agreed to help. "I figured asking for one was too much already, and it wasn't small," he replied and she turned to look at him. "Well, I like you," she replied.

He was about to say something but Talcen and Ticcen disappeared with a snap of her fingers. "And as for the rest of you," she said, looked at the pale green horde of mindless undead. "Your time in slavery is over," he said as her body erupted into pure blue flames and exploded outwards.

None of them were sure what was going on. For Talcen, time had resumed but the two of them were back on the tower and watching the blue fire expand and wipe out the enslaved vampire constructs in a rapid fashion with no visible source.

"Okay who was holding back on the magic?" Amanda asked. Nari was sure she just threw the weapon off the tower to help the two of them that were now standing beside her. "Not me," Nari said and was confused.

Thodon watched as the endless line of mindless monsters exploded in black fire right in front of him, also his hearing was fine. Everything was oddly looking up right now. He turned around and saw that everyone was still alive, more or less.

"Well, whoever had that trick up their sleeves, I just have to say maybe you could have led with that?" he said, but immediately realized that by the look in their eyes that they were just as confused as he was.

"These two fell off the edge not a minute ago and then they were back up here. I don't know what's going on," Nari said and shrugged. For a quick few seconds the idea of the golem was pretty much forgotten at the sudden turn of events they had just witnessed. Talcen was about to say something about Xy showing up, but he changed his mind.

"I don't remember. One minute I was on the ground and the next I am back up here, we both were," he said. "All I remember is hitting the ground and thinking I was finished," Ticcen said and didn't quite understand what happened. The world just wasn't making any sense, as if she missed something important.

"Guys, the thing, it's coming this way," Talcen said as he pointed in the direction of the golem. Sure, enough it actually was coming in their direction.

"I guess it has to do all the dirty work itself, this is so weird. Anyway, we are going to have to fight it. Keep your heads and your distance and you might make it out of here in one piece," Thodon said and the others weren't exactly sure how they were going to win here.

"Alright, let's get out of here and go take this thing down," Nari said and was the first one to jump off the wall. "Alright, follow her I guess," Thodon said and the others did the same. There was no way Thodon was going to fall from that distance and be fine. "You forgot that…oh never mind," he said. He teleported to the surface and appeared in front of the five of them in a white flash with the turret gun.

"I'll go first, I have no idea what this thing can do so I'll try to get it to attack. Watch and learn everything you can, alright?" Thodon said and tore the turret gun off the stand it was on. Before the others could say anything, he started to walk forward. "I think I want to be a Golem Hunter when I get out of here," Nari said, she was impressed by his willingness to go first into the fight.

"Don't kid yourself. Golem hunting is a dying profession. There hasn't been a new golem made in over a hundred years. In ten years or more there won't even be enough left for it to be a thing anymore," Amanda replied and Nari frowned.

"Born too late for all the fun," she replied and was saddened. "Don't worry, you could always be a Unicorn hunter. Those things are never going away," Amanda replied and Nari shook her head. "Hell no, those things are too much for me to deal with. I couldn't even handle a fake one," she replied. Amanda just shrugged.

"Guys, he's almost there, come on let's get closer in case he needs help," Talcen said and started to follow him. The others did too, Ticcen was confused at his sudden change of confidence. Before he could barely shoot one of the golem's minions, now he wanted to fight the source of their trouble and didn't have a single shred of self doubt.

The others didn't know him that well and just thought it was part of his personality, she, on the other hand, found it very unlike him. It wasn't the time to ask. She walked forward with the others, weapon in hand ready for anything she could imagine. It worried her that this thing might have more tricks that none of them would ever see coming. It was an unsettling thought that needed to be shut down.

# Chapter Twenty Eight

Thodon approached the purple eyed demon that showed no interest that some-one was approaching him. In some ways this golem was just like all the rest. A full machine and that's it. In others it was one of a kind. He would find out what made it tick after he dismantled it. Either way he was going to make enough to live on for a long time with this hunt, maybe even retire.

Although he wished that he would have called in some back up at least. Four neophyte vampires didn't make him feel very confident in his chances.

That gun he held in both hands began to spin to life, a second later it began to fire. The bullets slammed into the large black skeletal thing in front of him and to his horror, he could see the bullets just bouncing off and random angles.

"Okay," he said in disbelief as the thing just kept its pace, unchanged, slow and methodical. Then Thodon looked closer, the bullets weren't hitting the golem at all, they were impacting with some kind of energy field.

"Oh, come on," he said and was disappointed in the development. He needed a new plan and then he came up with one on the fly.

"It has a shield, get behind it and shoot it in the back. Maybe it's only on the front side," he yelled out to no one in particular. He didn't care who did it right now but he didn't stop shooting just in case by some chance he was able to use the concentrated fire to break through the shield. Right now, that was his only chance.

They all heard the order, but none of them really wanted to go that badly. "Come on, it's our only chance to see if it has a weakness," Ticcen said, almost volunteering to go. Yeah, and it's a suicide mission, too," Nari suggested, she didn't know that but the chances seemed pretty high that this was going to be the case.

"Stop, I'll go," Talcen said, gripped that shotgun tight and started to run. "Wait!" Ticcen yelled but it was too late.

"We better get ready to do something in a hurry," Amanda said and watched him as he ran towards the golem, making a large arc in order to try and escape its attention. "I suppose you can try to get ready to die, but that seems like a tough thing to do," Nari replied as they watched. No one replied to that.

Talcen ran as fast as he could and was doing his best to avoid the bullets that were deflecting from the shield. The golem didn't seem to notice him, if it did it didn't react at all. He then realized that the weapon he had worked best at close range. The one place he really didn't want to go. He remembered the deal the Goddess had made with him and now there was no choice but to throw caution to the wind and hope for the best.

In seconds he was behind the monster and changed directions. The turret gun must have been a good distraction because it still didn't notice him. All the better, he thought as he ran straight at the back of the thing.

Jumped through the air to clear the distance between them. When he thought he was close enough to fire, he did so. The shotgun blast hit the golem in the back and caused it to stumble forward. It was evidence to everyone that there was no shield here, and it was the weak spot, at least right now.

Talcen smiled at this and he was turning to run away when the golem spun around at its waist with incredible speed and grabbed him by the throat with its right hand and stuck a silver spike through his chest. Everyone watched in horror as Talcen's eyes went wide with shock, then his body crumbled into ashes before them as if he never existed at all as his red essence flowed into the golem.

"No," Ticcen said quietly as she watched this happen. The golem turned right back around and continued to walk towards the remaining people. Thodon hated to watch what happened but right now he was going to do his best to make sure the kid's death wasn't going to be in vain. He drew back and tossed the turret gun to the side. It wasn't going to help him right now but he didn't want the golem to wreck it either.

"Okay you over grown dirt pile, we're doing this old school," he said, he had no idea what that meant and it sounded a whole lot better in his head just before he said it. He pulled his sword and axe out at the same time. The golem stopped in its tracks and seemed confused, as confused as a magical machine could possibly get as it tilted its head to the left a little bit.

Red magical runes on Thodon's black armor began to burn red and he was giving himself every advantage that he could think of right now. "What's all that?" Nari asked and pointed. None of them really knew, even Amanda was clueless on all of this stuff. "Who cares, let's kill this thing," Ticcen replied and started to walk forward, not one single plan in her head. All that was there was the rage, this thing had to pay for what it did.

"I think it reacts to projectile weapons with a shield, at least, that makes sense. Maybe we shouldn't bring our guns," Amanda suggested and Ticcen just threw her weapon to the side with no thought to it. "Sounds like a plan to me," Nari said. She didn't want to die and was afraid of what they had to do next.

Thodon knew the others would be coming after what it did and he also knew that right now they were just going to die, one at a time if they got in the fight. He wanted to tell them to stay back but there was no point in doing that right now. He charged the golem and it swung its left silver wrist spike down on him.

He raised his own blade and blocked it. The axe was moved up to block the other blade as it came at him. Even with his strength enhancements this thing's physical power was incredible. He was putting everything he had into blocking this attack.

Those burning purple eyes were too close to his own right now so he used the leverage, lifted himself up and kicked the thing in the chest with all the power he had. It was enough to send the golem backwards. It slid, but didn't fall.

It slid through what little remained of Talcen's ashes and sent a cloud of grey up into the air around the thing. Thodon tried not to think about it as he ran forward. His sword was blocked by the silver blade but the axe carved into the black golem's shoulder.

The purple energy sprayed like blood from the wound. The golem just ignored and was about to put the blade through Thodon's chest when a pair of hands grabbed the black arm and stopped it cold. Ticcen was there, risking everything. "Thanks," Thodon said as he struggled to keep the other hand from getting free. She didn't reply as she pulled the arm back far enough to allow Thodon to jump back. Once he did she did the same thing too.

"How do we kill it?" she asked. "Dismemberment is the best option we have left," Thodon replied and this felt fine to her, it even made her smile. The golem looked between the two of them then something hit it from behind. Nari used her left fist and considerable natural strength for a surprise attack.

Thodon wasn't going to waste the chance and he threw his axe as hard as he could. The blade buried itself in the top of the golem's head and that purple fire exploded in all directions. Instead of falling, however. The golem reached up, pulled the axe out and threw it right back at him. Thodon's eyes grew wide. That blade hit his shoulder and glanced off the armor. It fell to the ground and so did he.

The golem jumped forward, its blades extended, ready to kill Thodon when Amanda slammed her shoulder into the thing's side, knocking it away. "I don't think so," she said and picked up the axe as she ran forward. In one fluid motion she brought the blade down on its left hand and severed it from the arm as it was starting to stand up. It swung its arm up and the purple fire hit Amanda in the face. She screamed as the strange flames caused her skin to burn and backed off.

Instead of having a silver blade on its left hand, now it had an endless magical flamethrower, somehow that seemed worse. The gash on its head and shoulder had long since repaired themselves, but the severed hand seemed to be lifeless now. "If dismemberment is going to be the answer, I think we're going to need a better method," Ticcen said as she and the others backed off from it.

Thodon couldn't help but agree with that. It was the only sure way to take it down for good, but maybe there was a better way to do this, he was starting to come up with a better plan.

# Chapter Twenty Nine

"We can't win like this. We need to retreat," Nari said and Thodon couldn't help but think she was right. "Yeah, I have an idea but we can't do it here. We need to move away from here and back to where all of this started," he replied.

"No, we can win here, if we run it'll never stop. We already have one hand off, we can win right here," Ticcen replied and her anger was getting the best of her. "No, we can't win here. That fire is going to fry us before we can even get close. Let's get out of here," Amanda said, still holding her face. Thodon was ready to run. "Follow me to the wall, quickly, we can teleport out of here," he said and Amanda and Nari abandoned their places and started to run towards him.

The golem was not going to wait. It turned towards Ticcen and started to walk in her direction. She was away from the others and deemed an easier target because she was alone. Her eyes grew wide and now reality was setting in. The heat of that mystical fire could be felt from here and there was no question of what to do next. She ran as fast as she could towards the others.

The golem jumped to cut her off as she did and landed right in front of her. Then it stuck that burning torch of a hand into her stomach. Immediately the purple flames rose through her body. She didn't even have time to scream as the flames consumed her leaving nothing behind in mere seconds.

Thodon had seen enough and teleported all of them back inside the fortress, it was by no means safe, however it made more distance between them. "Both of you get a bloodstone," he said and they both grabbed one and bit into it. Amanda healed up instantly and Nari felt better. "I can't believe they are both gone," Amanda said and was shocked, her imagination didn't allow for this much loss but reality forced her to believe it.

"I know, but we can't stay here. We'll mourn them later," Thodon said and it was the only thing he could say. The door to the gate started to burn with the purple fire and the silver blade was slamming against it. "Okay time to go," Nari said. Thodon teleported them all out with that same white flash just as the doors broke open.

The golem watched as they disappeared. It knew where they went. The thing turned around and started to walk away, completely ignoring its severed hand as it did.

# Chapter Thirty

Thodon and the others appeared on the black shore of the lake. "What are we doing here?" Amanda asked and Thodon looked around. "This is where it came from, we are putting it back," he said and there were a lot of things they didn't understand or know about the situation but all they could do now was just go along with it.

"What's the plan?" Nari asked and Thodon sighed. "This thing is too dangerous to be found by anyone and we can't let it leave here. My plan is to put it into a stasis bubble and throw it back into the lake. Hopefully it will stay there until the world ends," Thodon said and the plan sounded too simple and easy. Nothing so far was working out like they figured it should.

"It'll be here soon. You can leave if you want but I would recommend staying here. It won't chase me like it will you," Thodon said and the other two didn't have anywhere to go. "We're going to stop it or die trying," Amanda said and really didn't know if she meant it. At least she sounded like she did. "I'm with her, we'll take this thing down. I'll be the bait for it," Nari offered herself.

"Sounds good to me," Amanda said and Nari looked at her, she expected a little resistance but instead, there was none to be had. "Alright. When it gets here you, well, you're going to need to let it get close," Thodon said and sighed. "As close as I am to you now," he finished. Nari looked at the distance. It was easy to see that this was well within the reach of any of its killing methods they've seen so far.

"I understand," Nari said. She knew that she really didn't fit in anyway with vampire society as it was. If she died, it really wouldn't have been so bad. Death was going to be a nice vacation. "Once it gets this close. I'll hit it with the stasis field. Dive for the water as soon as you can," he said. He needed to make it sound like she had a chance to get away from the thing. She nodded, neither Amanda or himself expected her to live through this.

"I'm glad I got to know all of you," Thodon said and smiled. It was true. They were good people and he had been way too harsh with them most of the time. He felt sorry for that.

"When all of this over we can celebrate somewhere, honor our lost friends," Nari said with a sad smile. She knew she wasn't going to get any farther than right here.

Amanda smiled, put her hand on the giantess's shoulder, smiled. Then she turned and walked away. Thodon nodded to her. This all felt like a grim situation, however, he was going to do his best to make sure the killing stopped here and this thing's freedom was put to an end. He turned and followed Amanda into the thick trees.

Nari was alone now. The only sound around her was the quiet waves of the black water lapping at her feet and the still air. Any minute now the nightmare thing was going to come crashing through those trees and attack. Time when she was just standing here felt as if it each second felt like an hour. The tension was only going up. Where would it come from, the trees, the side, maybe it would just teleport in and stop wasting time.

Nothing, whatever it was doing, it was taking its sweet time doing it. Maybe the thing knew that there was a trap. Could a machine like that really know anything more than it was programmed to know? It was impossible to know for sure. But there was always the possibility that it was just lumbering about at its extremely slow pace all along.

It never was in a hurry before why would that change now. Nari's mind began to run in circles as she did her best to keep her guard up.

"Come on out you stupid machine, I'm right here," Nari said into the night hoping it might help. She was tempted to tear her pendant off and grow to her normal size. That might ruin the plan and there were no telling just what kind other horrible tricks it would have up its sleeve. Then she thought she heard the sound of crackling energy somewhere in the distance. She looked around but didn't see anything that had changed.

No, it had to have known something was up. This was too obvious of a set up. Nari looked to her right and saw Thodon and Amanda running in her direction. Sure, enough the Golem was right behind them. Her eyes grew wide and she realized that everything had just been ruined. She had no idea what to do now.

Did she stay where she was, did she move. All she could see was the panic in their eyes as they ran towards her.

Nari started to move but Thodon waved his arms back and forth and understood it was the international signal for something. The plan was still on, she supposed but didn't know or understand how yet. This didn't look like much of a plan to her.

Then when the pair of them were half way to her. They both turned around and charged at the Golem at the same time. Nari ran forward the two of them and watched in horror as Thodon threw something into the sand just in front of him.

"Throw us in the lake, now," Thodon screamed as a clear ball of energy appeared around the three of them. The golem, Thodon and Amanda froze in place just as they wrapped their arms around the monster, holding it back. It reminded Nari of a horrible snow globe, or still life art on display but realized that there wasn't much time to think about it.

She took her pendants off and quickly wrapped it around a tree branch nearby. Almost immediately she grew to her natural height of seventy feet tall with a burst of light and fire walking bac. The energy sphere looked small from up here.

It was clear that was no way to release them without breaking the field. And they'd both die at this range if she tried it. Nari reached down and picked the energy bubble up in her left hand. It felt like static electricity against her skin. Taking one last look at it, she tossed it into the lake.

The stasis bubble hit the water with a splash in the distance and sank beneath the waves sending all three of the prisoners to the unknown depths, likely for all time. Nari realized that she was alone now.

She reached down and carefully snapped the branch where she hung her pendants and immediately she grew back to her nine foot tall size.

Nari clasped both of them back around her neck and was immediately overcome with a hundred different emotions at once. Glad to be alive but, on the other hand, the survivor's guilt was powerful. She couldn't stay here anymore so she turned and started to walk back to where she hoped the path waited for her.

# Chapter Thirty One

Nari walked alone in the dark for what felt like hours. She expected some kind of a trap to be sprung or something like that and if it did she would rip that pendant off and stomp whatever it was into dust. She was just not in the mood to deal with anymore nightmares. The place seemed to realize that, as well.

Then she came to an opening, no, the beginning of the place. The stage was still there, but there was no fire. No one to meet her, it was just as quiet as anywhere else in this cursed place. She just walked to the beginning of the path, but she was still alone.

She didn't care about anything this place had to offer anymore, home, or anything else and had half a mind to just walk into the sun the first chance she got. The other half of her mind thought that maybe she was left alive for a reason. What that reason was, however, there was no way of knowing yet.

"Well. I have to say I'm sorry," Xy said to her and she jumped at the sudden noise. "Easy there," she said and she had no idea who this was. "Are you another trap?" she asked and her hand went to her pendant. "No, not a trap," she said and slid to her feet from sitting on the stage to the ground.

"You're the last one. Everyone who came here died. That monster killed them all," she said and looked sad about it. "But you know, that Talcen kid and I had a deal. Sure, he didn't make it but the monster got put down all the same," Xy said and smiled just a little.

Nari had no idea what any of this meant, but she knew who she was now. Despite thousands of questions that came to her mind, she thought it was best to not ask them right now. This made her see everything in a whole new way, however. Everything must have been real.

"I'm altering the deal," she said, waved her hand. Black mist exploded from the ground, breaking the stage into pieces. The black mist took the shape of people and solidified into obsidian. It was the rest of the group, everyone she had lost there with the words 'For those who fight' engraved on the bottom of the pedestal they stood upon.

"I can't bring back the dead immediately. It takes time. In one hundred years' time, Boron, Talcen and Ticcen will emerge from those statues. I will free the Dwarf hunter and other vampire as well," he said and smiled. "You can wait that long to see them again, right?" she asked Nari and she almost smiled.

"Yeah, I can," Nari replied to her.

"Oh, the blessing to the winner. You're it, obviously," she said and shrugged. Nari was confused. "Don't you care about the others who were lost?" Nari asked and Xy's eyes flashed for a second. "Oh, I do. However, no one fought. No one stood up to the monster. They all waited in their safehouses and died. You were the only ones who fought back," she replied.

"But, Boron caused the problem. I guess I—" Xy cut her off with knowing smile. "Just say thank you and shut up. I got this," she replied to her. Nari didn't understand.

"Thanks," she said and he touched her shoulder. "I grant you all the powers of a true blooded Vampire Queen. Use them wisely, fairly and with compassion. Mercy is just as important and powerful as wrath. But never forget what happened here," Xy said and Nari felt more energy than she ever had before in her whole existence as a vampire. Her eyes went from red to white instantly, but she didn't feel a thing.

"Go home, you have forever waiting for you and can do anything you want with it. I will talk to you later," Xy said and the both of them disappeared.

Nari had many questions but she found herself back at her house, everything was just as she left it. But nothing would ever be the same ever again. It was a bittersweet feeling that she would have to live with for at least one hundred years. She only hoped that she could live life to the fullest until that day came. She really wanted to see them all again.

She knew she would, someday, however the future remained uncertain and the chaos in her world didn't feel as if it was coming to an end anytime soon. Nari had powers other vampires could only dream of and now she felt that if anyone could make a difference in the world now, it was her.

Ticcen

Dear reader,

We hope you enjoyed reading *Camp Stonetooth*. Please take a moment to leave a review, even if it's a short one. Your opinion is important to us.

Discover more books by Jesse Wilson at
https://www.nextchapter.pub/authors/jesse-wilson

Want to know when one of our books is free or discounted for Kindle? Join the newsletter at http://eepurl.com/bqqB3H

Best regards,

Jesse Wilson and the Next Chapter Team

The story continues in:

Red Mirror by Jesse Wilson

To read the first chapter for free, please head to:
https://www.nextchapter.pub/books/red-mirro

Lightning Source UK Ltd.
Milton Keynes UK
UKHW041054231120
373920UK00001B/88